Do You Want to Live, or Pass?

Do You Want to Live, or Pass?

JOSÉ OCTAVIO VELASCO-TEJEDA

Library of Congress Control Number: 2015901543
ISBN: Hardcover   978-1-4633-9954-2
                   Softcover   978-1-4633-9953-5
                   eBook   978-1-4633-9952-8

Print information available on the last page.

Rev. date: 21/05/2015

To order additional copies of this book, please contact:
Palibrio
1663 Liberty Drive
Suite 200
Bloomington, IN 47403
Toll Free from the U.S.A 877.407.5847
Toll Free from Mexico 01.800.288.2243
Toll Free from Spain 900.866.949
From other International locations +1.812.671.9757
Fax: 01.812.355.1576
orders@palibrio.com
701271

Books written in English by the same author:

Deluxe chimp
Indelible *Mark*

Book written in Spanish by the same author:

Anécdotas, Relatos y Notas Interesantes
(Anecdotes, Stories and Interesting Concepts)

Science fiction novel written in english by same author:

Quieres vivir, o ¿pasas? (Do you want live, or pass?)

G IVEN THAT FROM adolescence, Pedro Iturralde considered the vital importance of; *to be,* in relation to, *to have,* he proposed himself to achieve a degree in science, an interesting profession: a job that required the utilization of intelligence, master a musical instrument (trumpet), and one sport (the amazing, astounding and marvelous Jai Alai), that is, to pay due to the Greek thought: *healthy mind in healthy body.* He decided that, although without a doubt, having riches provides various satisfactions, in his appreciation, it is not worth to sacrifice a life − having a profession and/or accomplishing work −, that it is not to someone's liking, for the sake of making a lot of money. Still, knowing that an intellectual job, it is normally not well paid by far; the compensatory treatment of a job in sales, for example, is quite different, so he never repented at all, having worked on practically all of the possible technical interesting places, within the field of computation (software). This was especially true, during the beginning of the aforementioned era, when it was really necessary to know, and understand completely, the details of the functioning of the; *hardware and software,* in order to get results, from a computer.

In Mexico City, not too long ago, existed several spectacular ads that quoted; *A life, a body, an opportunity,* that is an obvious asseveration, and however, how unimportant results for the majority of Homo sapiens. Iturralde remembered a fragment that he read from a book, written by Dr. Luis Alberto Machado: *The Revolution of Intelligence,* the following comment related to Leonardo Da Vinci; who definitely took said axiom to the letter, and who was a genius: "the only man; that has managed to be all that anybody can be, simultaneously, according to his epoch". And even more, he was an exponent to it, in maximum grade, in everything and in each of the sciences, and arts, that he dedicated to. Should not all human beings try to approach as much as possible to such example? Why resign oneself to one, or very few activities, of small transcendence in our lives? "Was Leonardo a genius, that could master so many, and so different activities? Or, was he a genius, precisely because Leonardo proposed to master so many activities that turned him into a magnificent man?"

No doubt, that obviously Leonardo's great capability existed, nevertheless, had he not have the tenacity (and enthusiasm) to learn, to lay plans, and to create, in so many areas, his talent would have gone wasted away.

Fortunately, Iturralde is pleased with the utilization of his life, body and opportunity, but as it so happens, that in our world everything is improvable, great satisfaction would have provided him, *besides*, having achieved a scientific discovery of important consequences for humanity. And (in addition to the above) the maximum level of possible personal satisfaction would have been the achievement of virtuosity playing a musical instrument such as a trumpet, or *at least,* the saxophone. And to top it all, with a perfect ending, having had the total musical capability (harmonic, rhythmic, and melodic), not to mention, the creativity, and the musical taste, to arrange and to compose, for big Jazz bands (music´s *Gran Prix*).

If for someone that enjoys Jazz, that really loves good music, the listening and intellectual joy that this art provides, is unequalled, the level of happiness and satisfaction for the creator, must be unparalleled. Of course, all the above, without a doubt, takes a great dose of great talent. In his biography, Sergei Rachmaninoff himself, his favorite composer of classical music, refers to himself with this comment: "I have listened that people say that I have a lot of talent; it may be that that way, but I consider that perhaps 10% constitutes talent, but unlimited quantities of study and dedication (tenacity*)* **is** needed, in order that talent provide the awaited reward".

Pedro Iturralde likes complicated things, and he had the immense luck to find, in different stages of his life, a variety of some of the most difficult activities to dedicate to, that they are the ones that he believes

JOSÉ OCTAVIO VELASCO-TEJEDA

are worthwhile, at least, for himself, especially considering that one lives only once. And it is not, that he had been specifically looking for the complicated and complex activities to pursue, and dedicate himself to them. No, he only lives his life in totally normal form, but when he encounters one of these complex activities, his capacity of amazement shows up, and he dedicates himself body and soul tenaciously, with unlimited passion and enthusiasm, until he manages to master them, or at least attempts it, and he study each with all dedication.

In relation to his own education and professional life, he lived during the initiating and maturing epoch of computation, and he embraced the opportunity completely. That is, from the point of view that interested him, which was the solving problems as a programmer, systems analyst and systems engineer, a professional thinking life; that is, he was not interested in the activities of top management, and even less the sales area, where one can progress to attain wealth, but where the intellect required for these activities is of another type, of totally different reasoning to the required for the referred technical aspect.

Other important field of his concern, was the scientific and technological advancement that occurred during the XX century, and first decades, of the XXI, that provided the ground for awe and wonder, and guided his study towards mathematics, and other branches of science.

Regarding his musical taste, he came across the most complex musical genre, what other that Jazz? Due to his luck, his older brother was a Jazz enthusiast, and when listening the very first Jazz album, he became instantly trapped by its intellectual beauty and sonority. Accordingly, he bought a Hi Fidelity equipment, and started collecting only the very best virtuosos available. Thus, he was able to form an enviable music treasure, while also attending to, as many as possible, jazz concerts of consequence. Later on, he enjoyed presenting Jazz seminars, when he consider himself well prepared to such challenge.

Iturralde, a very good amateur Jai Alai player, who had managed to win several championships. In one occasion, in a championship being undefeated, already having won two games, his front player, Konrad is awarded a contract to become a professional player at the Philippine islands, and without having the minimal education to inform Iturralde, he departs. Evidently, since the teams play in couples, Iturralde loses the following two games by default, and becomes eliminated, with plenty of probability, to earn two national championships, especially important because he already was sixty four years old. Probably, had he achieved it, it could have been considered to earn one Guinness's Record.

During another later game, two months after, when the score was even, with just two points remaining to finish the game, being the match so much competed, and having that point lasted for more than two minutes, when Iturralde was returning a very difficult ball "scratching" (the left-hand wall) and close to the Jai Alai court's posterior wall, and no wanting to return an easy ball, to his front opponent, Iturralde exerts an extreme physical effort, that causes him an intense cardiac infarct, which provokes his collapse, as if fulminated by a ray, wounded to death.

Immediately, all the players take off their *cestas,* and they rush, to help, his collapsed friend. Iturralde finds himself conscious, but with an extremely intense pain, in the cardiac region, as well as, in the jaw, almost unequivocal evidence of a cardiac infarct. Iturralde asks one of his friends to reach for his cellular phone, in which memory, are found his cardiologist's telephone number, and his wife's, and requests to call them immediately, and announce them what has happened. The cardiologist Dr. Laurel suggests that they do not move him, that they place him on a comfortable and covered position, in order that he is warm. Although it seems to Iturralde an eternity, in reality, only half an hour has gone by, when Dr. Laurel arrives, takes an electro cardiograph, and in the meantime, provides Iturralde with a sub-lingual tablet of Angiotrofin, in order to reduce his almost unbearable pain. While this happens, the paramedics in the ambulance arrive and wait for the doctor's orders, who at this moment is calling to the hospital, so the angioplasty specialists team get prepared to receive Iturralde, due to his very precarious status, he has to be attended immediately. By then, Iturralde's wife has arrived, and talks with the doctor, who communicates her, than the health of her husband is extremely delicate, but that at the hospital, right now, a great specialist's team, for this type of situations, awaits for him.

At that point, Doctor Laurel, indicates to the paramedics that they proceed to take Iturralde to the ambulance, and then to the hospital, where he will be attended. Iturralde still conscious and with a most tolerable pain, due to the received medication, and mostly of all remains calm, when seeing towards his beloved wife Lulu, to his cardiologist and to the ambulance and his tranquility persists (as always has been) to accept what comes. After all, he knows that, since death is inevitably, that there can be not a better death, that showing up, while doing what you love with extreme passion. Already in the ambulance, accompanied by Lulu, to whom he comments that it is the first time that he, fortunately, is being transferred, with the siren at full blast, in this type of vehicle.

In scarce thirty minutes (considering the sluggish transit), the ambulance arrives at the hospital, Iturralde is taken to a surgery ward, where several studies of all types are performed, and finally an angioplasty, incredible technique, which involves inserting a catheter into an artery at the groin, which leads to the four heart arteries. The result evidenced that, the four coronary arteries presented serious obstructions: three of them were clogged seventy percent and another one, one hundred percent, this last obstruction was provoked by an aneurysm that was obstructing the aforementioned artery.

Very serious situation that required an immediate surgical intervention, for which, one of the first steps was to verify the existence of, at least, five liters of O- blood (a rare type), that was not the case, which is why it was urgent to obtain that precious liquid, as soon as possible. For that matter, calls were made to some radio stations, as well as, to relatives and friends in order that they donate the requested blood. At eleven o´clock that night the endowment of blood requested by the hospital was fulfilled, thus, the operation was scheduled for nine o´clock of the following morning. Doctor Alcocer who was the assigned surgeon to operate Iturralde, visited Iturralde that evening, in order to explain, in full detail, what the indispensable surgical intervention exactly consisted of. It would be necessary to remove the four clogged arteries and to substitute them, with stretches of veins, in good condition, taken from the legs.

The probability of a successful intervention was good, but it consisted of a high risk operation, due to the implicated organ, and the damage that had resulted from the infarct. The surgeon's explanation and his conversation yielded confidence to Iturralde, and thus, he said so, to doctor Alcocer, telling him in turn that he was calm, and the fact that he had no more than a light fear, and the fact that he was prepared, if death awaited for him. That way, with great tranquility, he said good-night to his wife and fell asleep. Around two o´clock in early morning, another intense pain in the chest wakes him up, similar to the first pain, so the nurse calls doctor Alcocer, who takes around an hour in stabilize Iturralde, who now painless goes back to sleep. Iturralde is taken to surgery at eight o´clock in the morning, not for an operation, but rather to practice a new angioplasty, in order to be able to determine what damage stemmed from that new infarct, evidently, a professional adequate measure.

The new angioplasty reveals that the aneurysm has disappeared, leaving the aforementioned artery that was containing it, totally clogged, which changes radically, the medical steps to follow. No longer a bypass operation is to be performed, with the risk that it implies, the medical commendable intervention to follow involves placing *stents* on the three surviving arteries. That way, the doctor communicates the new procedure to Iturralde. Iturralde is transferred again for a second angioplasty in only two days. Thus Iturralde says good-bye affectionately to his wife and to their three children, and he enters the surgery ward. There, doctor Meadow, doctor Alcocer and their assistants welcome Iturralde and give him words of hope. They give an explanation of the procedure that they will follow, saying that he should not be worried, that everything is going to come out well. Iturralde replies to them that he is calm, and that in the worst-case scenario, is not afraid of death, although of course he would feel sadness, for no longer returning to see his family. He takes note that the date is March 28, 2002, he wants to know about the date of his possible death.

That way, they begin to administrate the required analgesics, and Iturralde senses that he is falling asleep, and all of a sudden, appears in front of him, a very bright tunnel. He remembers that some people have said that, a tunnel is seen by some of the people that suffer clinical death, which is why he concludes that he has died, but however, he feels great tranquility and inner peace. The tunnel seems to be of a great length, but he cannot insure it, since time does not seem to pass in the aforementioned dimension.

Quietly, he reaches the end of the luminous tunnel, and he comes across a very beautiful vegetation in front of him: enormous plants with flowers that never he had seen or even imagined, since the colors that he was seeing were of true high definition never seen, and everything is perfectly well-kept. Iturralde turned around to see the white and bright tunnel, where he had arrived, which had disappeared completely. Given that Iturralde always had liked science, immediately he tried to find a lead of where he could be at. He thought of a worm tunnel, and that he traveled to a distant point away from the solar system, or even of the Milky Way. Could this be any one of the eleven dimensions that are proposed by the String theory, a Parallel Universe, or else; another place like, for example: Heaven? How could he know? Could he?

At that point, he listened to an internal voice, which was answering his question as follows:

– Welcome to "Integritas", you got to this intervening place via a worm's tunnel, which is provided to all humans that fulfilled certain minimal requirements, that refer to their behavior at their land, that I will comment to you at a later time, if you care to know. The humans that behaved adequately, only will be able to see the aforementioned tunnel when they are conscious at the hour of their death. In the event of a fast death, although they will not be able to see the tunnel, in the aforementioned moment, the tunnel will be created so they can be transported to this place, the one that you find yourself in now. Sometimes, if it does not happen the clinical death, some humans are able to see the formation of the aforementioned tunnel which they can see as an extremely intense white light, when they are about to die, but the medical team is able to resuscitate them.

The mentioned worm's tunnel is personal, utilized normally only once, and it is created utilizing the dark energy that you find in all the universe, and that the terrestrial scientists not yet manage to understand, or what can it be its use. This is only one of its various applications. In this place the "souls", although it is possible to recognize people, because they show an image of their face during their lifetime. The face can change, that is, it can look younger or older according to the epoch that they want to remember themselves. Any other question that you have only requires considering it, and I will answer it to you gladly. Do you have any other question?

– In fact, yes, I do: answered Iturralde, who are you?

– My name is *ÓMICRON* and I am the *polymath,* –in order that you understand–, I am the supreme expert scientist *in several* disciplines, of the Universal Conglomerate *PUD*, whose initial letters mean: Parallel Universe Design, and I reside normally in a very beautiful place, the Parallel Universe *HQ*, that is where the head office of our Center of Cosmic Investigations resides, inside a black hole.

I have an office in the Venhea Galaxy, from where I am getting in touch with you. While visiting this office, I wanted to see the list of the characters that were arriving, and when *listening to* your question, I decided to answer you, and it is the first time that I do this, given that nobody before you, had asked such a question, with such clarity and so scientifically.

Our civilization has developed a sort of a very advanced telepathy that enables such exploits. You find said galaxy in your same universe, and relatively close to Integritas, which, in turn, is located in the Andromeda Galaxy, in one of its arms, in a very similar planet to the so-called Earth. Since you liked to read science books, you know that the estimated duration of the universe (where you lived), by the scientists Fred Adams and Greg Kaughlin, is close to 10^{100} million terrestrial years, which is basically correct (at present, have passed only 10^{10} million years). When that long time has concluded, Integritas will also disappear and all "souls" within, *will appear* immediately in another, –also *temporary*–, parallel universe (unless my collaborators and I have found the solution to the entropy problem, which I believe to be imminent).

What you call heaven, we call *Agones* since it is the competition par excellence, the one and only that has true significance, because it is at stake that; when finishing terrestrial life, like in another uncountable planets that, by means of evolution, have achieved that intelligent beings happen, it is the eternal permanence extremely pleasurable, or quite the contrary.

– Did you say that you live inside a black hole? Incredible and inconceivable, what you are narrating to me and for all humans, *ÓMICRON* please continue.

– Indeed, that is what I said. You have some knowledge of black holes, for you they would be lethal, but not for us. Similarly, what you call *soul*, here we call it *Dasein,* which means *being there,* owed to the fact, that when someone is admitted here, is for all eternity. The human invention that you call *hell*, here we call it *IPU* (INTELLIGENCE POORLY UTILIZED), which finds itself replete of politicians, avaricious industrials, pederasts and of course chiefs of all the churches, and another types of criminals, that caused great damages and extreme poverty to his fellowmen. By far, the pederasts priests, will suffer the more severe grief, the multi-billionaires, presidents and popes, where the damage in quantity and quality was enormous (with scarce exceptions). You will like to know that; given your preoccupation, in very fraudulent investigations such as: the murder of President John F. Kennedy (and his son and his brother Robert), as well as, the 9/11 farce, all of the involved will receive immense eternal suffering. This human garbage have very grave charges, in addition to his endless avarice, the manufacturers of arms, but most of all, treacherous traitors and murders on a large scale, to his own country.

– How pleasant to learn, that all the barbarities and injustices that happen on earth will be punished, it proves to me aberrant that no justice exists and no payment of damages will result. For your previous comment, I give myself account that, contrary to what a corrupt and accomplice mass media proclaimed, several government agencies were involved covering up 9/11, that is, it was an internal job, was it not?

– Of course it was, and it is evident with only observing and making a comparison of a building collapse by normal causes, and as it gets destroyed by means of an implosion or explosion; thousands of tons of cement turned into very fine dust, thousands of tons of steel conveniently cut for its easy transportation to China. That way, – just observe–, that is enough to know how it was done. A simple deduction indicates those who could be the only capable to do it, –since they have the control, the motive and means –, evidently only the federal government and its controlled agencies. Everything seems to indicate that, in order to know the truth (of almost any important event), the only possibility is to see the news, when it has just happened, at that point the control of all of the mass media, is not total, and worthy witnesses provide declarations that the following day, will no longer appear. The commentators that day, said what they saw, the following day they will change their description of the facts, to lies dictated by their bosses in the news agencies. That is verifiable for those who have same-day recordings of the dramatic and terrible event.

– Say *ÓMICRON*, how well-informed are you about these events, that I would swear that said happenings, were either unimportant, or unknown to you.

– Our civilization has the means, and the interest to know all that happens in all of the universes, that we have designed and started. This event, in particular, interested myself in excess, I could not believe that the people did not react, demand to know the truth, and punish the culprits. I am glad that the American architect Richard Gage, has formed the movement *9/11 Truth*, where he has managed to convince and obtain close to two thousand engineers and architects that; *do not suck their thumb*, and they are asking for a serious and independent investigation. Additionally, like you know, they have gather several groups, such as; scientists, army officers, firemen, honest politicians, Hollywood's artists, etc., but they have not yet, achieved their purpose

– Also Omicron; the really important issue is; that there are proofs of the many motives and profit that several groups of traitors, that they benefitted by the form that the great majority of the ineffectual persons to accept the evident truth; by utilizing –the scientific method–, which strongly suggest the use of Nano–Thermite. Not to mention the very severe crime; the very quick removal of evidence material, immediately after the event, before carrying out an investigation.

– That's right, Iturralde, going into the whole bag of tricks of the tragedy, tens of *inexplicable* situations find themselves, that they form an unending chain of facts that show a very sloppy planning. Many governments, right now, feel so safe that the people will believe anything said, and viewed in television, and newspapers, that they do not worry about the story of some criminal event committed by them, so they have become completely careless. Another very clear example is the magical bullet of the murder of president John F. Kennedy. Do you remember *the magical* bullet that accomplished several impossible spins to cause injuries to two people seated in not aligned places? Not content with that, at a later time they killed his brother; Robert Kennedy and, later on, the president's son. And absolutely nothing did happen. With those precedents, the Governments take more confidence and they become more careless in their criminal future planning and doings. Do you agree?

– Yes, Omicron agrees, with the aforementioned suggestion the fact that they are right now accomplishing it, perhaps, will be able to prove the existence of a certain amount of justice. The governments' power, form its own force, by controlling all of its organizations, that in turn control the population and *besides*, because the majority of the people is not interested in committing themselves to a cause, which implies time, and besides setbacks. Especially, at the present moment, people have become very selfish, they do not put in time neither for patriotic events, nor for the family. They are only interested in friends, talking or hearing *music* all day long in his cellular phones, and at night seeing the television set projecting some news bulletin; –irrelevant news–, the crimes of the day, or any other deformed news in relation to its veracity. And to finish the day they see films, some few that are worthwhile, but the vast majority, pure trash. Thinking, reading some book that increments knowledge, or examining facts; like 9/11 and taking action, that is for others to do, if it is what they want, but let me alone with the aforementioned suggestions, they argue.

The punishment that I impose for all that did not make good use of his intelligence to do good things, is the following; they might have enjoyed very much at their land, and provoked a great quantity of bad deals, but that will be at the expense of what awaits for them in eternity. The worst punishment that occurred to me, that was neither cruel, nor violent is: the accused; those who did not want to utilize their intelligence either wasting it, or even worse utilizing it to do evil, have procured for themselves, their eternal permanence in the *IPU*. Their minds will attempt to utilize their intelligence to his peak, but that enormous effort will be able to produce no thought at all, they will be unable to concentrate, neither to pay attention, nor to have fun. They will bc like being always dead, but conscious, −a very weird situation−. With a lot of potential activity and big desires, but they will be unable to accomplish any action. Total inactivity. For all eternity. There is a general punishment for all of them, that resides in the fact that, they will have to hear, the distinctive mode of your civilization, mainly, pop music constantly, integrated by three participants: a drummer that will beat the battery merciless (that is, normal), a guitarist with his hideous electric guitar distorting at maximum volume (impossible decibels to produce with their amplifiers and terrestrial loudspeakers, and a vocalist of frightening dumb voice (also normal). Only playing the same song all the time, and to an unbearable maximum quantity of decibels.

Besides, there are especial punishments for certain types of malefactors of inconceivable wrongdoing, such as:

a. The greedy; their only activity will be to count, −by means of their memory only−, infinite fortunes, cent by cent (pennies), for bankers and avaricious insatiable industrials, and every time that they make a mistake, they will have to begin counting everything again. Is it not, a great form to *enjoy* their avarice, for all eternity?

b. The politicians, religious chiefs and priests; will have to hear an only discourse repeated for all eternity. Like the majority of their *postulates*, it will be completely discordant, illogical and full of lies. Is it not a great form to *enjoy* their demagogy?

c. For the murderous criminals and drug traffickers; they will have a permanent *imagery* of themselves torturing their relatives and friends. This is one of −the painful punishments that we apply to these perverts' Dasein. If being extremely harmful, was so much enjoyable, that very same thing will apply *virtually* to their loved ones, or at least to their close buddies.

d. There is a very especial punishment for the pederasts: when the sexual activity (intercourse) ends, if it is tried to continue with it immediately, it produces great annoyance and scorching pains. Their eternal punishment will be to have the aforementioned unendurable pain, more and more intense sensation, in their Daseins. This is the other only painful punishment that we have, because to damage innocent children, to such a degree, they have to pay their grief more severely, than everybody else. And for the ones that committed a combination of the above-mentioned crimes, the combination of the payable grieves exist. I clarify that the physical pain no longer exists after death, but they will feel a terrible and increasing pain (a great deal worse than the physical pain) in their soul, or rather, their Daseins. Now then, for the children and young people of good behavior, that the wicked adults misguided them into evil, these will be judged with the correspondent benevolence, and inclusive may receive a punishment not for all the eternity and less severe. As you can verify, here benevolence and impartial justice exists.

– In effect, Omicron, I agree that those are the worst punishments, that they can attain, how cleverly devised. I would go nuts in a couple of minutes, to hear the infamous existent pop music, played at volumes of madness, commented Iturralde. In relation to the more severe punishments, I consider them, perfectly appropriate and worthy of the grief that they will receive, for such atrocities that they committed.

– Now then, for the humans that lived generally doing good things, or even, causing a certain amount of damage to another humans, which showed certain grade of selfishness, within a tolerable given scale, I, ÓMICRON will evaluate the time for them in Integritas, that I will determine that proves to be absolutely just. From there its name; Integritas, that is, pay, indeed, in enough benevolent form, for their human partially undue behavior, during their lifetime on earth. Indeed, there are no prayers in the universe that may reduce this waiting time in *Integritas*, not to mention the *IPU*.

– This, I see as a purgatory equivalent, which seems very reasonable. Now that you talk about prayers, what is your opinion about our multiple religions on earth?

– ÓMICRON continues; astonishes me, that humans could have learned science, with plenty of approximation, and that each time they approach a little more, but the complete knowledge of everything that they go into, although they will never know anything 100 %, and however, the greater part of the terrestrial civilizations, have had and have, so obtuse and harmful beliefs, as all religions are. Is really amazing that they believe that some god require millions of prayers and unending sacrifices offer themselves, and that in return, god listens the aforementioned prayers, and rewards them, with miracles. God never would have permitted, that the earth to be in the situation in that humans have deteriorated it. The evil and the catastrophes in the universe you lived in, exist for the simple reason that no planning was exercised.

– You already made a comment to me about punishments, but do you have in like manner ÓMICRON, contemplated especial rewards for the humans that really utilized their capable intelligence to their plenitude?

–Really, you came up with a good question! Here we have an equivalent to what you call; the Nobel Price, although, it is evident that it is of another proportion, and of another dimension, as I will explain it to you now: one reward for the scientists and two for the musicians exist. This is due to my appreciation, that these are the only two activities, that I consider that have an eternal relevance, and the fact that, besides they are the only ones that can keep on having a good time for situations that I will mention to you in some other time. The reward *TDS* (*Thinker Distinguished in Science*) has been received by all scientists, those who accomplished any significant contribution to science, or else, to technology. All scientist that I notify in science of destructive or harmful technology, of any type, does not receive this reward, but the adequate punishment, according to reasons explained to you previously. All prize winners, that are several thousand, receive the same reward exactly. Here does not exist anymore the envy, which different levels promote. The aforementioned reward consists in that their Dasein, is established a very deep satisfaction for all eternity, they find out, that their lives, where they made good use of their intelligence, to their capacity, it was worthwhile to live it. They need not monetary rewards, applause, or diplomas. It is something personal and intern, but of immense value for those who receive it. More than enough for their effort, all of them are highly satisfied for the aforementioned recognition. In other words, Einstein, Newton, Darwin and the inventors of the transistor, etc., evidently with very different contributions weight, there on earth, here the fact is, that their intelligence, was utilized for the benefit of their fellows humans.

– Without a doubt, on earth, this would have seen itself like a certain amount of great injustice, because each contribution, provided different achievements and cost-reducing advantages, but your point of view is also understandable. No longer they have to struggle to compete, right now, in this wonderful place. This is in relation to the rewards of science, what do you tell me, in relation to the rewards received by the musicians?

– In such case, it is called *TDM* (*Thinker Distinguished in Music*). I believe, that it turns evident, that the granted aforementioned rewards concerns exclusively to Classical and Jazz musicians, due to the fact, that in those two musical genres, where the intelligence is utilized, in levels that *are worthwhile*. The recipients of the aforementioned Classical rewards are, as you would suppose: Rachmaninoff, Bach, Beethoven, Mozart and all the other contributors of beauty in *sonorous intelligence*. With regard to the very brilliant instrumentalist that played the music created by the composer, since they were *only* interpreters, they receive the IDM (*Interpreter Distinguished in Music*). When the recognition is given to Jazz musicians, where Jazzmen are basically instantaneous creative, due, not less, to the improvisation, the reward is named IDJ (*Improviser Distinguished in Jazz*) and I can name to you; Chet Baker, Frank Rosolino, Art Pepper, and hundreds more. Studying where the spark of improvisation for the first time took place, I learned that: Mozart and Bach were the most prolific originators. I bet, that you did not believe, that I would have knowledge of your civilization's detail, not so?

– No, of course not, you leave me overwhelmed, but considering it with great detail, a civilization like yours, if it can create universes, you can make almost anything. Your Bach and Jazz mention, remind me of a comment that a great artist of chamber music mentioned that: "Bach and Mozart were masters in developing themes. I am sure than once they were able to come off of their creation, and learn how to Swing, they would be able to *seat* with Shelly Manne's quartet, and to have a good time, ad infinitum".

I agree with you with such recognitions that match with mine. Being intelligence is so important for you, I want to comment about a book; *The Revolution of the Intelligence,* written by the Venezuelan thinker and writer; Luis Alberto Machado, by chance, do you know about what I am talking to you, asked Iturralde? I am not surprised by your great knowledge of events, and of your interest in our planet. Due to difficult reasons to understand; improvisation disappeared completely within classical music, and it was taken by Jazz to form one of its principal characteristics, also, it is non-existent in any other musical genre.

– Of course, that it does not come by chance, all of the valuable books published by your civilization, are in our virtual libraries and they have been read by our civilizations, as we have managed to change our civilization level. In order to become what we are, knowledge of all cultures, something that we have acquired, of which we could have made good use of it. This happened, certainly, when our civilization was still of low profile, but we moved rapidly up to better levels. You, who right now are experiencing our basic form of communication, are becoming aware of our capabilities. I will mention to you and you will understand it immediately, since you dedicated yourself to the computation field, all your life, what multiprogramming means, and about the multiplexor channels. The principal difference is, that in your experience, the aforementioned techniques were starting. What I am talking about, is the commented techniques incremented by several degrees of magnitude. Concretely, we can accomplish any quantity of simultaneous activities. Reading any civilization's library does not take time for us at all, in the meantime, also we can perform all the activities that comes to our minds. Now you can go on, with your story about Machado.

– How fantastic, that so incredible exploits that you are able to perform. I, with a lot of work, was able to locate him in Venezuela, and asked him for authorization, in order to be able to utilize fragments of his text, for which he granted verbal permission, I found such material fascinating, which was utilized in two books, that I wrote linked in relation to the development of intelligence.

– How adequate on his part, thus, he is not a selfish person, he lends his thoughts with his readers, ÓMICRON comments: as for the books that you wrote, do you want to comment me, in relation to them?

– Of course, what a great honor, Iturralde answers. The first one is called: *Deluxe chimp*. The first part of the book, establishes the principal dangers that threaten our society, in the immediate future, which are quite a few, and each one of them is very complicated to *solve*. They are not really problems, all of them form a body of threats, called in fact; predicaments, which do not have solutions, but only consequences that will happen, independently of the actions that the societies, or all the planet do. There, I comment the virtues and defects of our species, where I qualify it, under the title of the book; the most that we can aspire to achieve. The second part of the book, is where the important concepts of Doctor Machado come into play. According to him (and I agree with him completely), intelligence involves relating, which is basically why he demands to learn this, to practice and to accomplish, consistently, his Relational Method, which will allow improving the intelligence to a large extent, possibly, in several orders of magnitude.

It is evident to Iturralde that practically all of the governments of the planet, are interested in having controllable citizens which have the closest to a void opinion, thinking citizens would get organized and would not tolerate absurdities and or the aforementioned governments' injustices.

Only one documented case of an exception exists. In Venezuela, during the mandate of President Luis Herrera Campins, Doctor Luis Alberto Machado was named: Secretary of State for the Development of Intelligence. Sadly, when taking possession the new government, immediately that Secretary office disappeared. Doctor Machado's merit, to be called to occupy so important position, is directly related to his book: *The Revolution of Intelligence*. Fortunately, I have the said book, as one of my favorites. I go back to reread it, from time to time. A quotation from his book follows:

"In order to attain any individual or collective goal, the first thing that it is required is an unyielding conviction that the foreseen goal can be attained. It is possible, than even obeying this requirement, the goal, may not be obtained. But, certainly, without obeying it, it will never become successful".

Is it not, Doctor Machado referring to tenacity? Iturralde believes to have, at least, the aforementioned attribute, which has allowed him to acquire, all of his achievements.

— I also agree with Doctor Machado´s perception, he is correct, indicated ÓMICRON. Was that book read, by most of your planet's inhabitants, was it?

— No, unfortunately, it failed to click into the populace. Its publishing ran out, I know it because, I wanted to give it to my relatives and friends, as a present, but it was already unavailable.

— It is a pity and a tragedy, without exercising great intelligence, a civilization cannot survive. Please go on, with the comments about your book.

— Sure, I am delighted. In the second part, I describe a specific *Method of Relation,* which I advise to be utilized at the schools as early as primary schools. A necessary complement is the study of science, to be an ineludible companion during all the educational stage. In conclusion; I propose in the book; the Development of Intelligence, Science and Wisdom. It seems to me, that it is an indispensable trilogy, in order that a civilization may get better, not to mention their survival. Without intelligence and wisdom, science will, in all likelihood, be carried to absurdity and to destruction, like for example; the design and construction of the atomic bomb, and worse still, the hydrogen bomb.

JOSÉ OCTAVIO VELASCO-TEJEDA

– That is correct, you are exactly in the aforementioned stage, when the civilizations level zero, where they run the bigger danger. That happens every so often, where civilizations destroy themselves, at precisely that stage. It seems to me, of first order your way of thinking. Our thought in some very remote moment was that one precisely. That teaching and his implementation were vital for us. Apparently, your book has neither been read by enough people, nor by the governing body, is not so?

– The book was not published until very recently, since no publishing house took interest in publish it. They told me that it is a book of *broad knowledge,* and therefore they were not interested in publish it. Furthermore, I took the bother to visit twelve of the embassies of the principal nations of earth, asking them for an interview, directly with the ambassador, in order to offer him, the method that I found, so that their countries may utilize it. All of them are stubbornly dreaming, in the absurdity of *unlimited growth.* Neither country gave me any appointment, nor did I receive an answer to my letter. Luckily, finally, I was able to publish it, paying for its publication.

– ÓMICRON answers back, I see, sad situation, I congratulate you for your attempt to wake them up of his dream of: *unlimited growth* of all of the inhabitants of a limited planet. It is the most that you managed to do, therefore you can be more than completely satisfied. What does your second book, is all about?

–The second book title is: *Listen, Learn, and Enjoy Jazz,* and it is a disclosure about this great art. This book has not gotten into print, for similar reasons. The part that Doctor Machado contributes to this book refers to the *tenacity* that said *Method of Relation* proves to be effective only if it is taken seriously and practiced with passion. He presses the point that once a method works well, it was found that it is required to practice it daily, in order to achieve the mastering of it. In no way, is a simple process, like everything that it is worth in life, you are required to sweat, display effort, dedication and constancy. This book is a great recompilation of information for anybody who wants to learn this musical genre in depth. It summarize my experience of over sixty years of my life listening to it uninterruptedly. Once that I decided to present seminars, I gladly had to learn a great deal about the details of its origins and its particularities.

– As you say: *there in no free lunch.*

– I recall that before you did make a comment about the soul, what can you tell me about it?

–When humans are alive on earth, they have no spiritual attribute, what you call yourselves; *soul,* which does not exist. The *Dasein* takes shape in the following way: at the exact moment of death, the memory of all his/her life (including when they were babies or old men, even the ones that suffered Alzheimer), stored in each brain, does not get lost forever, rather, it is stored in the mentioned *Dasein,* and it is going to have everlasting life. It is for this reason that it recalls all of his relatives, experiences and events that turned out to be pleasant, and no longer it will remember any event that was unpleasant. Its knowledge and pleasures will never disappear, but quite the contrary, they will continue to have a good time with an intensity, in the highest degree, and will be able to continue learning, ad infinitum, about what right now they know, and of any other matter that they could not learn on earth, including music, like in your case.

– What wonderful news, one of my more valuable passions were to learn, especially about science and music!

– The difference is: that you no longer learn practicing an instrument. Here, once you acquire the musical knowledge on harmony and counterpoint, only is enough to think which instrument do you want to play, and which notes, and immediately you will listen them in your *Dasein*, to use the correct term in this place. As if this be not enough, when entering in the *Agones*, there will be unlimited quantities of intellectual new activities, infinite in number and in depth, this, in addition to what right now is found in *Integritas*. As you can see and check now, and most of all afterwards, the *Agones* is, anything but boring, in this way, I answer the question that you asked previously.

– Which are your origins, where do you come from, ÓMICRON?

– Long ago, agriculture was discovered and implemented, but in a conscious, careful, limited and nondestructive form. My ancestors bodies, although with totally different nutrients required –unlike the terrestrials–, in like manner ate such food; like fruits and vegetables (also very different from the terrestrial), which is why they utilized the aforementioned process, until more advanced civilizations (referred later on) canceled altogether that subject completely.

Our forefathers, used to live in what you call Andromeda galaxy, in a system similar to the solar system, in the planet Nebus. They were in a situation similar to the terrestrial, but they reacted on time, our scientists alerted the population regarding the existent problems. The heads of all nations joined together all of the leading scientists and took very drastic decisions which were taken as obligatory for the entire population. I imagine that there were those who did not agree, but the order was implacable. Our civilization was at stake and that way the governments understood it. The punishments for the violators of said new super strict standards were very severe, but I know that they were disobedient in very few occasions. Our forefathers had their good share of more intelligence than terrestrials. Also we unrolled atomic weapons, but we did not have them in the quantities that now exist on earth. Every weapon was destroyed, and wars came to an end in our civilization. Atomic energy was utilized in our reactors, in order that, they provide us with energy. But as soon as it was possible for us, we stopped utilizing them, due to the problem of the unsafe residues.

At our beginning, our progress was very slow, all that we were utilizing was done practically by hand, there were, for a long time, no machines. We did have oil, and coal, like it happened on earth, and we used plenty of those resources. Nevertheless our population was in check, –no more than two billion–, and we never allowed any damage to our air, water, or land. That was considered, and enforced by law, as a criminal act, almost as bad as killing a person, therefore, no contamination existed. Our scientists discovered electricity and magnetism and they got the same theories basically that your most notable scientists. I could be able to name (I will not do it, because his names are unpronounceable for you) equivalent scientists to your Archimedes, Pythagoras, Newton, Einstein, Darwin, etc. They came to the same findings than your counterparts on earth, in the principal laws and scientific themes of importance.

They managed their natural resources, very consciously, so much that, they had enough, and they were able to visit all of their planets, of their corresponding star. Near the end of said adventure, they had developed very concentrated energy fuels, which, indeed, unable them to the mentioned space adventure and permitted the possibility of much farther exploration, that is, star wise explorations. Given that, it was a massive energy consuming civilization, our scientists did not have any choice, except that to learn to utilize the energy of our star Sirrus, in the form of extraction of the most efficient energy. There did not exist another way to obtain energy, in the required amounts, and without energy, we were on the brink of extinction. Finally, we started building machines, everyone utilizing star energy. But that quantity of energy was, to all effects, insufficient for our progress, at some stage of our advancement. Our scientists applied themselves with all his intellect and the entire population's governmental and civic support to achieve an advance, unprecedented, in the form of utilization of light and heat of our star. Their population was very stable and very well educated, all people knew mathematics and science. Needless to say that, music had been agreed that demonstrated unprecedented development to significantly increase intelligence. At the beginning of the manufacture of our machines, our solar machines were like toys, with little purpose and potency. But, little by little, larger energy solar cells were possible to develop, which went evolving exponentially in the production of energy and decrease of size. At a later time, those machines were enormous, no contaminating and, with potency in excess for any work.

When miniaturization was discovered, later on, our tiny machines accomplished medical wonders which permitted that our health and longevity triggered to unsuspected levels.

Regarding our instruments and music, evidently they are unlike any of the terrestrial music completely. It is more different than the occidental music and the Chinese music, in order that you understand me. From the very first time that I listened to classical music, I was captivated. When I first listened Jazz, it was an embracing

JOSÉ OCTAVIO VELASCO-TEJEDA

exhilaration, so I revised our literature and learned all about it. Accordingly, I was able to convert and download all music available, so it could be reproduced by our sound machines. In fact, terrestrial music, of the mentioned genres, is the only music that I listen to, all the time. Our forefathers and even more advanced civilizations were not able to invent equivalents to the European harmony, the counterpoint, not to mention: the art of improvisation. In like manner; the sonorous quality and variety of your musical instruments, is music insuperable and irreplaceable. Unfortunately, your instruments, are not usable for our civilizations, given our so different physique. I am interested very much, and have laid plans for producing universes that could have the bases for good music like your terrestrial, which I consider ideal. One question that I ask myself is; if the quality of music that exist on earth is so magnificent, why is it that almost all that is produced and heard in the latter decades, is in charge of *musical primitives?* I do not understand such a waste of taste and intelligence. There appears again the lack in the application of intelligence, which as I commented before comes with its price tag.

With respect to mathematics, it proves to be very similar in some aspects and very different in another ones. The similarity occurs when the branches are equal, for example, say, geometry. But each planet has uncovered different branches than, of course, they do not agree with the other branches discovered in other planet, to name some example, the Boolean Algebra that your people, already know, did not exist for our forefathers type 0. It was invented or discovered, as you prefer, until we became civilization type I.

Medicine, although having to do with very different beings, apply to the diseases caused by bacteria and viruses, it seems to be that, they inhabit in any existing universe. There are enough proofs, that life appears eventually and independently in planets, where they have appropriate habitats in any universe, where they take very different shapes. It is to say: that evolution shines like an insurmountable *law.* That appears sooner or later, as from the smaller virus, you encounter mutations than are doing step by step into more and more apt animals in the course of millions of years, adapted to their environment, and finally, they manage to develop intelligence. Therefore, the vaccines were similar and hospitals and similar doctors, treating similar diseases in both planets, to extremely unlike patients.

The universities welcomed their pupils rather young and when graduated, they already were considered responsible of their own acts. Postponing the aforementioned process artificially, was not considered appropriate. This premature education trains young people to form big scientist rows. Every pupil, from his first year of school, leaned music (very different from yours), since this subject assisted profoundly with their learning of other subjects, especially the ones, related to science. When memorization was required, this turned out well, by means of the relation with some object(s) to exercise the intelligence. The more important subjects were; our idiom, mathematics and all the exact sciences. What is more important is that; from the first year of school, they were taught how to learn. They learned to examine postulates, documents and theories and to criticize their strong and their weak points. They had to prepare their own theses and to defend them in public. They should have learned how to be excellent orators. Those were their basic learning tools. They learned how to become more intelligent. They learned how to learn. By themselves. They could take a new concept or unknown matter, to examine it and understand its essence or function. That is, we prepared them for thinking, making good use of their intelligence each day better. One of the exercises involves giving two themes or concepts to the pupils, apparently not related, but that however, when thinking deeply, they are. It is this task of finding such unsuspected relation(s) (and frequently you find others), of great intellectual enhancement. The pillars that catapulted our development, in order to, be able to climb civilization levels, to get to our present-day level, were those.

− How interesting chats we are having, Ómicron, little by little, I learn better the type of advances that permit the rising of the civilizations, according to their advancing with respect to its type. Could you modify the respective constants, in order that, planets where life will eventually exist do not form big oil deposits, since this apparent blessing ends up producing contamination and climatic change that produces great damage to themselves, as it is happening on earth, and also, preventing that agriculture may exist?

– Look, Iturralde, granted that oil is the result, of millions of years and of millions of animals decay, that stored in their bodies the energy of their star, and that way they formed enormous deposits when getting buried, I cannot do anything with regard to this matter, since the part of the physical constants that I can manage, do not control your mentioned question. In like manner, I cannot avoid that agriculture may happen in a civilization, if the inhabitants discover it, and they decide to utilize it. But allow me to make a comment to you, that, in fact, there is nothing wrong with both of those benefits that the planet has given to them, as a present, to its inhabitants. The problem, resides, as well as, in many other aspects, not in its use, but rather in its abuse. Let me clarify myself; if the population suitable for the planet should be; one or two billion inhabitants, at the most, and instead of such quantity, they allow the population to grow exponentially, to its present-day level of more than seven billion, and even so, they continue on the increase; it is not that oil and agriculture are harmful, as such, you make them harmful for its absurd unlimited consumption. Well utilized, – with the limited population –, as stipulated above, it would have been beneficial for your civilization for several millennia. As it would have been useful for us to our initial civilization, granted that we did not commit the same error that you committed. We come back to the same thing; a limited planet, cannot grow boundlessly, is it not something evident?

– Without a doubt. Only to fulfill my curiosity, I am convinced that CO_2, – causing global warming–, constitute a great problem and that, among another disasters, will cause floods due to melting of Greenland and even worse of the Antarctica. Is such scientific perception right?

– I have to answer you, as a scientist, the proof points to, that it is, more than likely, if the tendency continues that way. Nobody; neither governments, economists, politicians, industrialists, well, nor even the citizens want to stop living a comfortable life, they are unable to accomplish the least effort to avoid consumerism, waste, to recycle and to use again. And that way, there is no form, to avoid such catastrophe.

– Ómicron, asked Iturralde timidly, is it possible, to get to know you, in person?

– I would like to please you, but there exists a very strict rule that has a clear wise intention, which impedes that Daseins, while they find themselves in *Integritas*, can see us, let alone, living together with anyone of us, that is, with members of our civilization. I am sorry to deny it to you, but I can do nothing with regard to this matter.

– Thank you anyway.

–Iturralde was unable to continue to be quiet, without asking Ómicron this question–. What is your opinion, regarding our attempts to contact more advanced civilizations than ours?

– In relation to the terrestrial attempts to achieve contact with more advanced civilizations than yours, I assure you that it is a nice try, but, most likely, you are not going to obtain good results for various reasons:

a- Advanced civilizations, do not have the slightest interest in contacting newer civilizations, since they know, – incorrectly–, that they will not learn anything from them. Our civilization is an exception, we are the most advanced, and we are glad with the results obtained, due to our enterprising attitude, and as universe creators, we became very interested in the study of the evolution at different scenarios, the new parallel universes, which we are able to create.

b- Imagery and sounds from your TV, and radio stations, that you have been sending to space since approximately sixty years, demonstrate your civilization grade of dullness, when showing an almost total lack of intelligence. And anyway, the delay time is really enormous while getting signals to some very distant planet with advanced civilization, of some type.

– Iturralde, thinks; thanks ÓMICRON, now I have another question, of which, I always wanted to know the answer, and it is related to your previous answer. Certainly, you can help me; in the book; *Hyperspace* by the scientist Michio Kaku, he presents the classification that the Russian astronomer Nikolai Kardashev, gives in relation to the grade of the technological advance a civilization has acquired, as follows:

"A *civilization type I;* is that one that controls all the planet's sources of energy. This civilization can control the climate, prevent earthquakes...This civilization has finished the exploration of the solar system".

"A *civilization type II;* is that one that controls the energy of the sun. This civilization's requests of energy are so big that directly consume the energy of the sun to move its machines. This civilization would initiate the colonization of local systems of stars".

"A *civilization type III;* is that one that controls the energy of a complete galaxy. Its needs of energy are so great, that they control the energy of thousands of million systems of stars. Probably they dominate Einstein's equations and space-time can be manipulated at will".

Our terrestrial civilization, on the other hand, finds itself in category *civilization type 0*, almost initiating space explorations, consuming and close to deplete its fossil fuels, worrisomely damaging the ecology of the planet very fast, and at this rate, no longer could they may aspire to achieve a change of category, they could not be able to survive for a lot more time.

– I can answer this question very easily indicated ÓMICRON; it turns out to be amazing to me that a human, the chimpanzee's very close relative, may happen to know scientific issues, such as theories, hypothesis and even conjectures that, to a large extent, come out to be true. As your scientists asseverate with all truth, they will never be able to know the totality of the truth in any respect, however, each time they will be closer to the truth, decreasing the level of uncertainty, or of error in their knowledge. Strictly speaking, in fact, there exist not three, but four civilizations' categories, being the *DUP* and I, ÓMICRON, its higher *executive*, those who are civilization *level IV*, the higher category of civilization that, we believe, may exist and whose only limitations are: we cannot know the very distant future, our time's arrow advances only forward, the same happens in all of the parallel universes, and the more urgent and harmful matter is controlling, reverting or even better to impede entropy, which is to us still impossible to realize. But curiously, because you could be a witness of our long pursued goal, which I am about to receive, the confirmation that, for the first time, one of or created universes, has been freed from entropy. Until now, all parallel new universe that we managed to start, necessarily end, as dead universe, with the so-called heath dead (calorific death), where finally all process of any type comes to its conclusion. Uncounted with energy, all process, of all types, become suspended, not even a bacterium can subsist.

– Absolutely fantastic, for us, to imagine a civilization type I, proves to be difficult to believe in its existence, but the one that you have achieved, where it is not only possible to utilize all of the energy of an universe, but to be able to create universes, you become far away of all understanding, except for me, that right now, I am here and in conversation with you, at least, I know, for certain, that it exists: – a *civilization level IV* –.

– What do you need to create a parallel universe?

– I, like any scientist, in any parallel universe, have to have experience and knowledge regarding the results of every combination of constants, that I want to be applicable for each new universe, which I obtain, evidently from experimentation. Given that I, ÓMICRON and our civilization is eternal, it is not important than each one of these experiments takes time that is outrageously enormous. In order to obtain measurable results, this does not have the least importance for us. Regarding the civilizations' levels I, II and III, there exist enormous quantity of all of these categories. The great majority of them, with levels that, as Arthur C. Clarke mentions correctly, in his third law, where he affirms that: "any civilization sufficiently advanced is indistinguishable from magic". The results of many capable planets of the evolution of intelligent life, they prove to be ready for its civilization's destruction. Humans, they are not an exception, they are certainly, on the road to precipice.

– I believe to know the terrestrial problems, but which is your perception of our crossroad?

– There are, at least, four fundamental problems, that propitiate a presumptuous disastrous scenario:

The first serious problem is; the *avarice* that some, – relatively few –, of the aforementioned civilization's members cause destruction and exhaustion of the capability of the planet to preserve life. The rest of the population, blindly keep on with the destruction of their planet, without utilizing their intelligence, in spite of the fact, that they are preparing the killing of themselves and they do neither see, nor they understand it. They prove to be blind and deaf to the warnings that their scientists announce. They prefer to go on with their comfortable life, but that their aforementioned way of life and pleasure, instead of facing the very difficult situation, and trying to stop their civilizations very sad destruction in a short time. Their enormous commercial centers – Malls–, being built ad infinitum, in all the planet, and besides, their distant giant stores, that require the transportation of enormous loads of goods, instead of the local manufacture of all that is necessary. In this way, the large multinational enterprises continue to grow themselves more rich and powerful. All nonrenewable resources become exhausted, and the poor people become even poorer and more in disgrace. Do humans, have less intelligence than bacteria? Why are they not interested to preserve their own lives? What about the life of their children and grandchildren? Because they will suffer all grave consequences and will not forgive them, because right now, they are warned by enormous scientists' groups, since long time ago, therefore, they do not have excuses. Why do they play along with the shopping centers, businessmen, banks, politicians, governments and all kinds of advertisements, all associated with the destruction of the planet? What do humans have within their heads?

The second grave problem; is the total lack of interest of humans in utilizing and improving their intelligence, they are immersed in the promotion and enjoyment of stupidity, in a descending spiral that is taking them and their civilization in all of the important branches of life, to a level of stupidity and brutality, very inferior to their close next of kin: the chimpanzees. This certainly, is the cause of big discomfort for me, ÓMICRON, and which, will take a very severe penalization, that I have already indicated to you, in another part of our conversation. It is unthinkable to me, that the human being has not been able to utilize his intelligence to the full, all the time. I do not request that you do not have fun, but even fun should be intelligent, in no way, stupid, monotonous, or driven by instincts. Scientists have shown them all their discoveries on evolution, have proven to them, that the one and only thing that tells them apart, among all animals, *is the grade* of intelligence. Humans turned out to be descending from apes; with luck they got a brain of bigger volume, for totally fortuitous reasons, which allowed this animal a superior intelligence. Thus: *utilize it, do not be so ungrateful!*

Evolution, that by pure chance, achieved improvements through millions of years, keeps accumulating tiny changes, that somehow were helping the survival of the possessors of the aforementioned modifications to *design* the earth's most complicated being. Therefore, I do not forgive, under any circumstances, the voluntary waste, of the more important result of one of my experiments, this is, even for me crucial. Something unsuspected, the human brain, origin of civilization's first level; – 0 –, wonder that amazes, the universal scientist, ad infinitum. Although the intellectual capacity of a human brain is the size of an electron, in comparison with a universe, that would correspond to our brain, there, evolution has achieved the first step, to be able to keep on, to attain bigger intelligence. Therefore, the waste of a brain, seed of better brains, proves to be unpardonable to my requirements.

The third grave problem; the generalized incapacity of the human mind to understand: the mathematical concept of exponential growth. His mind does not manage to understand a geometric growth, where, literally, all of a sudden, the problem; *explodes on the face*, no longer allowing to remedy it, on time. But they do not understand it, because they are not interested in understanding it, several scientists, among others; Doctor Albert Bartlett, have explained it for years, without achieving that people take interest, take it into account, and take the necessary steps, at least, for reducing the problems of their planet substantially. In a video where the aforementioned exponential growth is explained, by means of a simple example; a bacterium lives on inside a plastic bottle and reproduces itself each minute, as from 11:00, in such a way that there will be at 11:01, two bacteria, at 11:03, there will be four, and so on; each minute the population doubles itself, and he asks: at what time will the bottle be half-full? The answer: at 11:59, that is; in only one minute, at 12:00, the bottle will be full. It is not then: that the problem explodes on them, *on the face?* But let's think that, a *far-sighted* bacteria, have taken into account, that something is going bad, and decides, at 11:58, to look for more bottles and she finds three more! How lucky! What a colossal discovery! Problem solved, right there, they have four times the quantity of bottles that they were having originally. For how long will they be able to utilize them? Two minutes: The four bottles will be full at 12:02. Certainly, Iturralde, given that you are a mathematician, you understand this concept. But, how many people understand it? How many presidents, senators, economists, politicians and multinational owners do? I assure you that almost no one, and if they understand it, but they do not change their behavior, then, their head is useful only to comb their hair, and to watch Foot-Ball games, or even worse, wrestling matches.

The fourth grave problem; lies in that, in general, neither they know how to distinguish between something vital and something important, I am referring to: know the difference between a problem and a predicament. They treat predicaments, as for example, global warming and the exhaustion of their valuable natural non-renewable reserves, as if they be problems and, therefore, they try to find solutions that do not exist. Humans, in fact, have a predicament that encompasses several sub predicaments, which present only various possible scenarios or consequences, which no longer have solution, they will happen, unless they may avoid them, in time. But neither politicians, businessmen, governments, nor the population worries about them. Their consequences, in all likelihood, will be very saddening and painful. I will put the following example, to distinguish such concepts to you: while a person finds herself grabbed to a branch, that is anchored firmly to a part of a precipice, this person has a severe problem, but she has alternatives; she can ask for help, she can try to go climb or to descend, she can hope that somebody can help her, with a rope. Those can be improbable alternatives, but they continue to be possible. If this person loosens up, she slips off, or loses grip, and she falls, her situation of a problem becomes a predicament. That is; an unavoidable consequence will happen. The aforementioned concepts are quite different.

It is lamentable that, unless that something, extremely improbable happens, or that they begin to act cooperatively and immediately and in a globalized form, there seems to be very slim hopes for that civilization. And the scientists that have tried to alert their governments and citizens with little success, you yourself that have had the interest to read and to study books, like for example, the book; *Limits to Growth* written by doctors Dennis and Donella Meadows, as well as their update, published thirty years after, where very clearly, show the very distressful scenarios based on studies (mathematical models) that predict, with plenty of probability that, almost inevitably, catastrophes will show up, and get worse, more and more, in a date not very distant.

– It is very clear to me, because it is my way of thinking and corroborates with the examples that you commented me, which should be sufficient for anyone to understand them. I am inclined to believe that it is simply laziness to think, one does not require the knowledge of space rocket science to distinguish it.

– Iturralde now asks: does another element, in the periodic table exists right now, that may produce thinking animals?

– ÓMICRON answers: we are making experiments with another carbon isotopes, because I am not satisfied with the obtained results, in the way that the DNA forms the recipe for the manufacture of the proteins required for the formation of the human brain, or in some other type of being, in the immensity of planets where life, of another totally different characteristics exists, because it is almost impossible for evolution, to repeat in the same way in another universes, in particular, regarding the number and type of nerve cells and of their interconnections among them.

We are searching for the Homo sapiens brain, to be *really* sapiens, or of any other similar animal that its turns to be a true intelligence, especially in the related to the utilization of his brain, for the easy and fast understanding, and utilization of sciences, the care of his planet, of his society and of his family. In like manner eliminating all negative inclination, especially the avarice, that is the principal cause of the terrestrial present-day problem. As in all the other situations where we require new experiments, ÓMICRON only wishes to change the basic parameters and quit. That evolution, by itself, without any additional *divine* intervention of any type, could produce all of the changes in order that the subsequent experiments proceed. It does not please me, at all, that when enough intelligence exists, in order that, a civilization progress, they finish destroying their planet and inclusive themselves. This answers your previous question, in relation to my intervention, in a parallel universe created with new parameters.

ÓMICRON additionally commented that, it seemed so absurd to him that, based in religious preaching, they believe that God created Homo sapiens, to his image. How can they believe such barbarity? How can they be so arrogant? I, ÓMICRON, who am not god, I want their well-being, but on the sidelines, not directly involved in some process, except for the initial, the one belonging to the definition of constants, but do not assume any kinship with god or with me. As Darwin, Dawkins and many other scientists explained very clearly, their closest relatives are the chimps, not god, or I. But that does not mean that they behave like apes, but quite the contrary. I recommend to humans, that they draw away from apes, – intellectually –, that they read lots of books on science, that they learn and not lose time in subjects without transcendence. Sports now are on earth more and more being followed by immense populace, especially the most dehumanizing; such as; boxing, bullfights (animal cruelty), etc. I do not want to imply that I disapprove all sports, only the type that I mentioned, as well as, living for sports. Terrestrial civilization should be thinking (and acting) in, how are they going to become adapted to their predicaments, in the least abrupt possible form, instead of brains being filled with sports for hours on end, every day.

– Well, regarding the just mentioned aspect, I was right, although I was educated by Jesuits, that they sowed in me the malignant seed of the religion, since my adolescence, I had serious doubts in relation to the great quantity of mysteries that they prescribed me to. Finally, one fine day, and after reading abundant books with regard to this matter, on science, and on the damage that religion has caused to our world, I already defined myself as an atheist. Regarding the amount, diversity and endless transmission of stupid sports, I was sick and tired of having to view that rosary of sports, that were compulsory to watch, since they appeared everywhere you were, and everywhere you looked, since the TV screens were almost everywhere.

– Which also had family impacts and with your friends, but you demonstrated intellectual courage, I congratulate you, for so brilliant determination. It requires a lot more courage to declare yourself an atheist, than an agnostic, but, of course, if you are convinced, you might as well, say it.

ÓMICRON continues: Another very important aspect that I want to correct, is the relative to the movement of the tectonic plates, since it causes grave earthquakes, as well as, the bombardment of meteorites and comets that destroy civilizations, or that at least, cause mass extinctions. In another parallel universe, I have done modifications and adjustments of the constants, in particular; with the intensities of the nuclear weak and strong force, and also, the force of gravity, and I expect that the result, in the mentioned experiments, be more satisfactory, in the aforementioned aspects.

As commented before, I am not pleased by the existence of entropy. Being a perfectionist, of course I do not like that disorders destroy the things that we have created, for other creatures in parallel universes. When we achieve that entropy no longer be applicable, we will be required to do other important adjustments, like for example that the totality of the population be fixed, since they will not be able to grow bigger than a certain limit, this will apply also, to individuals provided with intelligence, which have caused a lot more damage – over-population –, than the rest of the other sorts, which without the *un*intelligent intervention, maintain, normally, by means of natural causes a stable population. On the other hand, you have, as a fact, that a civilization educated appropriately tend to have small families, which do not produce over-population.

The things created by an eternal civilization, they owe therefore, being also eternal. But given that, there are an infinite number of parallel universes, really the bordering one, belonging to space, is virtually non-existent. ÓMICRON commented another experiment that they are accomplishing, in several parallel universes, still without positive results; that consists of chimpanzees typing at random, over and over again, generation upon generation, to see the amount of time that is required to produce, the complete Shakespeare's work, and in accord again with the calculations guessed by some terrestrial

JOSÉ OCTAVIO VELASCO-TEJEDA

scientists, the required time is, for all practical purposes, really infinite.

– Iturralde comments: Richard Dawkins, accomplished a very interesting intervening experiment in his computer, in order to show, how evolution works, – rewarding any change, small as it may be–, which helps the survival of its possessor. The sum of those small changes, through the passing of time, are able to design the most incredible organs, with spectacular functioning, but with equally serious defects of design. In one of the last books that I read; *Your Inner Fish*, by the paleontologist Neil Shubrin, he talks about our origins, and of how practically each one of our organs, is badly designed, since their origin is evolutionary, and dates of millions of years ago.

– ÓMICRON comments: the existence of intellectual absurd positions is for me inconceivable, like for example; creationists and the new fashion of intelligent design, that teach poor innocent children that are initiating their lives with beliefs based on lies and other aberrations at schools. As I know that you are very much interested in the evolution of the levels of civilizations, I will go describing to you, in several commentaries and in broad outlines, the more important advances of every level of civilization, but according to the few concepts that you may understand, because already in earth, there was certain advance in them, or at least your scientists were trying to go searching into themselves, and to take them to practice to be able to utilize them, basically for the indispensable generation of alternating sources of energy in the very deteriorated present-day civilization.

–Iturralde had oceans of scientific questions, which were requiring answers, which is why he began to think in them to ask ÓMICRON for answers and he presented them in the following form:

– I imagine that a type IV civilization's requests of energy are absolutely enormous, unimaginable for humans, therefore, from where do you obtain such quantities of energy?

– ÓMICRON began to mention the partial list of the sources of energy that Iturralde wanted to learn, with the following comment; I am going to mention some of which you would be able to understand, others, would be incomprehensible to you, for the moment, at a later time, you will understand them fully: *perpetual-motion machines*, which humans discarded, as impossible to fabricate, in fact, in your civilization they were impossible to design and, therefore impossible to manufacture, so you can grasp the idea: *several universes ago*, in order that you understand me easily, as a reference of the fact that, we utilized them in our simplest apparatuses ages ago.

– Thus, you, after all, found out that the perpetual motion does exist, you encounter how to proceed.

– In fact, and this happened when our civilization was still level II, when we still required of a complete physical body to accomplish work, which no longer, at our present-day civilization type IV, exists. It was in that epoch when my forefathers began to pursue several drastic changes. Given your inquisitive curiosity, I will give you a historic abridgement of how happened the adaptations, that no longer were, conveniently owed to conventional Darwinian evolution, but rather, totally designed and turned reality by our big scientists, that they achieved that our civilization managed to get to level III, and at a much later time, level IV, that now we occupy, and that, right now, we are almost totally convinced, that no longer a higher level can exist for any later civilization.

– Yes, it is impossible to think about something superior.

– The first decisive step that we took, was to place sensors on each one of the organs of our body, until at a certain moment, all the body's organs already had its specific sensor, and that way, we became aware regarding any type of problem, that was beginning to develop to the correspondent organ, in good timing. Then, when some sensor identified most any problem, we proceeded to activate the following procedure; to freeze the body, to devote it for corrective maintenance, and that way the physician accomplished an non-invasive operation, utilizing laser beams, –that you know–, in order to destroy, the totality of the damaged organ. Afterwards, an organ taken from our supply of organs, developed: via *mother cells,* we proceeded to replace the affected organ, from where they grew, as cells from itself, which work out as totally compatible, with the body where they were going to be transplanted. Transplanting as such, takes effect in similar form as angioplasty's technique. That is, it was introduced a catheter in the area where there it will be placed the alternate miniature organ (the aforementioned miniaturization will take place, immediately before is to be required). Once the catheter is withdrawn, the miniature organ grows to its requisite size, and all nervous and sanguine connections, and any other that is required begin to take shape.

– I understand, the body, or its equivalent, even when their bodies were completely different, than the terrestrial, were a great deal further perfect, than ours.

– The new organ's correspondent sensor, was included, also in miniature size, in like manner grows to its normal size, and it is in position, and all connections take place, in effect, perfectly well. On the following day, the patient´s temperature begins to normalize and, the patient recovers to become perfectly well, and in a few hours can continue her normal life. Once that the replacement of any damaged organ was possible, our quality and duration of life was increased in an exponential way. From then on, we began to tackle the problem of how to obtain our corporal energy. I refer myself to the way that evolution resolved this problem, given that it is not a reasoned solution, works out more or less efficiently, but far away from being perfect, which is why we focused ourselves, in obtaining one form much more efficient to accomplish this indispensable process for all way of life.

– On earth, very important advances in relation to the transplanting of organs turned out, somehow well, but this is another matter, you are talking about, the possible mass substitution of organs, even to achieve a body totally restored.

– Like good scientists, we began having minimal curiosity, that is, our first focus was to understand what evolution achieved, and the fact that other processes were more efficient, was evident. At that time, the quantity of energy provided by the sun (or any star) is of enormous proportions, and without cost (later we would find even bigger sources of energy), well then, that was the one that we were supposed to make good use of, our first focus was to obtain our energy, directly from the sun. Instead of taking foodstuff, utilize photosynthesis, just as plants do it.

– Curiously, I always ask myself the reason why the human body was not using, such as, the plants, the energy directly from the sun. You did not only considered it, rather you actually accomplished it.

– Thus, sometime after, we achieved several others advantages of the monumental scientific advances as they went progressing: we achieved that our skin had enough chloroplasts integrated, in order that, photosynthesis be the way to get direct energy from the sun, and therefore, we no longer needed to kill any animal, which is cruel, and contaminates our bodies with many toxins, cholesterol, parasites, etc. That way, from that very distant epoch, we do not know what eating is, that although we can read that it provided our forefathers a great pleasure, in like manner, it produced grave mortal diseases, a great deal of the time, like diabetes, obesity, heart attacks, various cancers, etc. That fine day, 100 % of them, were totally eradicated.

– It is very difficult to think, for me, while I was alive, in not eating, but your solution is grand, health *in abundance.*

– As from that one glorious day, our only nutrition consisted in water and the famous formula NPK (Nitrogen, Phosphorous and Potassium), that any person that knows of agriculture, or also, permaculture, or even knows of gardening, that the aforementioned elements (as well as, some other elements, in very small quantities), such as; Magnesium, Calcium and some others) they are fundamental for that plants can grow and survive. In like manner, the chloroplasts of our skin absorbed the carbon dioxide of air directly and that way our new form of feeding us, much healthier, and practically without cost, constituted a very large cultural advance, which was the great step to eliminate another grand mal, invented by the primitive civilizations, where money was invented.

– I had come up already with the idea that money, no longer should exist in advanced civilizations.

– This automatically eliminates the avarice, which changed completely our moral values, which gave as a result a totally just civilization, without neither rich, nor poor persons and with a reduced population in inhabitants' quantity, where each life had value, because it did not exist in excess. In like manner, the agriculture that has been a blessing for your civilization, also it has been a cursing, for the destruction that inevitably cause, and without measure absurd growth of population, it right away proved to be, totally unnecessary for our civilization. Speaking about avarice, I, as well as yourself, have taken notice that your civilization, has two severe consequences due to the overwhelming amount and notoriously marketing treacheries that run the economy of that planet, where the people with means has, as their principal entertainment, to buy, like there is no tomorrow. Furthermore, of all of the items bought, are designed to last the least possible time, and most of they are not reparable. So, the absurd avarice forces the nonrenewable resources to be depleted. That will provoke that the quick scarcity of most materials and the inherited problems to the following generations. Those new generations, I assume, will not forgive their predecessors of such infamous waste. We searched for worlds without predators, and having managed to eliminate the need to produce and to consume foodstuff, we consider that it has been a very important contribution to improve our civilization.

– The fact, that agriculture, in the beginning, was a blessing for the forming civilization, but it constituted a later serious situations; the unlimited growth of the population, among others, after ten thousand years, or so.

– This amazing drastic change, also resulted propitious, for a wonderful change that allowed us, to eliminate all of the necessary organs for the digestion of foodstuff, and that, represent also that our bodies, no longer produced the annoying and nauseating corporal residues. Additionally, it improved the population's health exponentially. As you know, the great majority of the diseases and infections are produced by oceans of intestinal parasites of all types, such as worms, and like the taenia, and protozoans, such as; amoebas, as they are taken within the foodstuff. The problem complicates itself, due to existing uncountable ill-mannered people that do not wash their hands after going to the restroom and in this way, the propagation of the aforementioned diseases is maintained by all those parasites, unless they may be exterminated. Indeed, when talking about parasites, you, humans, proved to be the worst parasite for your planet, since they have torn it apart, without mercy, and they have damaged it, and made it dramatic ill, and with great probability, just like the parasites that kill their host, they will perish or at least, the population will decrease drastically, and they will suffer deplorable conditions.

— I imagine, that anyone becomes accustomed to almost everything, inclusive not eating, that is, in advanced civilizations where they no longer need it.

— Our ingenuous solution, eliminated this situation completely. But there were still something to solve that involved eliminating the viral diseases. Ad hoc, our scientists eventually found vaccines for all type of diseases, what drove to a civilization 100 % healthy, free of all diseases. Once liberated of these fatal causes, we focused in getting rid of old age. For this arduous task, they searched and found, all genes implicated with degenerative, and inclusive, the suicide of our cells, that were caused by aging, at last achieving said process to disappear from our lives. From that moment on, we secured that we already possessed everlasting life, what a fortunate achievement, we took care of it, and we avoided all risks that, even remotely, jeopardized our lives.

— Something very important learned by me, everlasting life is possible, after all.

— Returning to the issue of waste matter due to digestion, by that time non-existent, evidently the private W.C. and public restrooms disappeared completely. In this way, our basic internal organs were reduced to the brain, heart, lungs, and all the senses, especially hearing and sight, which increased in exponential form our health, quality of life, as well as, our longevity. So, in fact, the only cause of death, was due to an accident. And, it is important to mention that, when death occurred, the cadavers neither did break down, nor it was necessary to bury, or to cremate them, simply it got disintegrated and evaporated without intervention of any one, which seemed us, the ideal solution to the problem of passing away. And therefore, the cemeteries also disappeared!

– It is impressive, even the problem of the remains was solved.

– But the energy that our bodies were receiving, by means of photosynthesis did not prove to be enough for our needs, as soon as, our scientists dedicated themselves to provide another efficient way to capture the energy from the sun into our bodies. This time, they incorporated very small and efficient solar cells in our forefathers' skin. With that additional quantity of energy that they were collecting, proved to be more than enough for their daily needs. A not too frequent request was to take sunbathing of not much duration to saturate the energy absorbed by their bodies, which was totally free. The space freed by all of the organs dedicated to the digestion, was occupied instead, in housing the battery, which concentrated all the energy received by means of photosynthesis and the solar cells that fed all the body, by means of strategic connections. The placement of this battery, was the one few causes of an invasive surgical intervention in the mentioned epoch, which in the beginning caused some problems, but in the course of time, was perfected and the implantation, just as a pacemaker, proved to be totally safe.

– That is, you, or rather your forefathers, made good use of the solar light and heat to one hundred percent.

– In effect, just after the aforementioned green counter-revolution, in order that you understand me easily, the so sought-after that your scientists never found: the Cold Fusion. At the time that your terrestrial pseudo-scientists Fleischmann and Pons deceived your true scientists, temporarily, by making they believe that they had achieved such discovery. To be fair, Fleischmann and Pons were in the correct clue when utilizing the electrolysis of heavy water acting on the surface of a Palladium's electrode, however, a much more deep study was required, in relation to their theory, that was the utilization of the combination of another isotopes, and another catalysts in the mentioned electrode, to obtain the desired reaction. To our scientists, this form to produce energy seemed impossible, even that intervening to the much more deep study of said process, and basically they met serendipity's lucky factor, and thus; they achieved cold fusion that finally yield the awaited fruits.

– I do not stop marveling, and I am only at the beginning in the knowledge of your wonderful civilization.

– Similarly, another important finding, which required extremely deep and advanced knowledge in nuclear power; fusion and fission and, in particular, in relation to the so-called; Higgs's Boson, which, on earth they continue searching in the big particle accelerators, which we managed to find very long time ago. Our forefathers have utilized the cold fusion to produce energy that we have utilized for various uses. Another discovery pertaining the enormous improvements in obtaining power transmission, is referred to our scientists finding the method for the utilization of *superconductivity* – at ambient temperature –, that, as you know, is the transmission of electricity without loss, which permits that electric currents circulate without any resistance, thus, indefinitely, which allowed its flow at highest efficiency in our bodies, industries and our cities, and so forth. Again, this improvement did not represent bigger cost, but quite the contrary. In this way, our civilization achieved each time greater available energy, for oceans of uses, and each time much more efficient, and at the same time reducing their costs dramatically. Another inexhaustible additional source for obtaining energy, that I already described you, continued ÓMICRON, is a form that also had been found by one of your great scientists; Nikola Tesla, who proposed providing energy obtained from space and could be perceived by a giant-sized antenna, free to everybody, which seemed unworthy to your associates absurd bankers and power companies, because it was unable to be connected to a current meter, to each user, that project never would come true (avarice again).

– Yes, I read about such discovery, but I never knew if it was something possible and real or not.

– No doubt about it, the source of energy found correctly by Tesla, was dark energy, which could have been used by your civilization, but that was perceived by our forefathers and utilized successfully from time immemorial. In this way, our sources of energy increased in several orders of magnitude and without cost for our citizens. This could have been accomplished by your people, and that way could save your planet, but your billionaires businessmen' avarice and your corrupt governments, made sure to eliminate that possibility.

– Thank you very much ÓMICRON, I will get in touch with you later, answered Iturralde.

Iturralde told himself; since I am going to be here a very long time, I want to find out about this place and what can be done here. And wanting to experiment about the way of existent communication at his new home, he thought; I want to see my former schoolmates from high school, and immediately, in front of him, there was a vast space where he found big tables, identical to the restaurant where the anniversary parties took effect. He found the tables busy, with young people in great quantity, and at the thought of getting close to them, in that precise moment he was there.

At that point, Iturralde took a look at what he could see of his body, particularly to his legs, where these would be supposed to be. In like manner, it happened the same thing with his arms. His deduction was immediate; really, right now, I am supposed to be dead, although my mind works, I no longer have body at all. In other words, the famous spirit seems to be that, after all, it exists. That way Iturralde began to acknowledge his former schoolmates, to whom he went saying hello affectionately. That curious greeting was only mental, simply, it was necessary to consider it, and in that form, simultaneously it was transmitted from *Dasein* to *Dasein*. Given that Iturralde knew computation on earth, he tells himself, at last, I can work in mental multi-task form, and I can communicate with them, by only considering or desiring it. And there were all the members of high school, but also, what was amazing, is that, it could be perceived that all of them, had the face corresponding to the age when they went to high school, just as he had been informed. He saw all their faces handsome, that is, any one of them flawless, and although they did not have clothing, they did not fail to look "normal", an impossible sight of being described. It could be said that they seemed like ghosts, with his very real face, and the rest of their body very tenuous, that is, similar to apparitions. Now, in front to his former school companions, they began to chat about their memories, of their professors, the Jesuits came to their memories: Maurei, Fernandez Moreno, Palomares, and so forth. All of them kept remembering the jokes and mischievous conduct of each one, and all laughed for a long while. All were very happy to be reunited in such a nice place. In that moment, if it was that the time concept existed, he thought about his family on earth, and in this occasion, nothing happened. Well, this business about obtaining what one desires, apparently only exists for this place, and it is not possible to get in touch with people on earth. However, this serious setback did not bored him, and he felt no sadness at all. He asked himself, and he deduced that in this place, no longer such sentiment of sadness exist, that, belongs to the terrestrial dimension.

That thought was confirmed by ÓMICRON who commented:

– Due to the existent distance between the Galaxy of Andromeda and earth, – approximately to 2,5 million light years away –, and having the light speed (*in this universe*) a limit of close to (only) three hundred thousand kilometers per second, according to accurate knowledge obtained by the terrestrial scientists, the communication between these two points is impossible (you will learn that, this uncomfortable limit of the velocity of light, no longer exist for our civilization), and on the other hand, in this place no longer sadness exist, in the least. In like manner, depression, solitude, hatred, boredom and all negative sentiments that existed on earth, no longer exist in this place. All thoughts in this place are only positive, and also, right now you will learn that intelligence does not have limits here. This is the reward that ÓMICRON offers to the people that utilized his intelligence to their understanding's best. To the big performers of music and science, given that they made good use of their intelligence to the full, they would continue to be in Integritas a short time (relatively speaking), depending on what they deserve.

Iturralde desired to accomplish several other tests: of all the interesting activities that he liked on earth, on which of them, will he be able to reestablish contact? What can you do in this place? If this is going to last for all eternity, I hope that it will be worthwhile, and not as the heaven that was pictured by religion, that is: a bore. And that way he began to remember the beautiful things of earth, the ones that impassioned him. Well, let´s try it, he said to himself; he wanted to share his sojourn here, and now join all of the Jai Alai players that provided him with emotion, joy and incomparable happiness during his life. And immediately it appeared, before him, the complete; "Hall of Fame" of Jai Alai professional and amateur players. They were, among others; Amuchástegui, Berrondo, Echeverría, Elorduy, Gabriel, Guara I and Guara II, Larrañaga, Muguerza, Solana, Unamuno and everybody else. Iturralde recalled the most spectacular game, that he ever witnessed: Guara I (front) and Guara II (back), against Solana (front) and Elorduy (back). He remembered that it was an extremely emotive game, where Elorduy played in the back position, not his normal front position. Interchanging positions, at that level, was very unusual – the playing abilities required are quite different –, but it proved to be, one of the best games that he witnessed. The game ended with a score; 30-29, winning achieved by Solana and Elorduy; that score marks the closest competitive game. Elorduy featured several spectacular (and "miraculous") plays which were invaluable, especially during the last point, that way meriting the victory. That game was so intense, interesting and well played, that the whole multitude reclaimed the players back to the court three times, similar to a classical music concert, where the featured musician(s) are acclaimed very intensively, when the audience appreciates the beautiful, faultless, and passionate performance, rewarding all the actors with several standing ovations.

At that point Iturralde thought about going back to investigate about the characteristics and achievements of level III civilizations, because he then formulated the following question:

– ÓMICRON, I would like to know about the technological and social advances that your existent civilization, somewhat similar to ours, could go progressing in a way absolutely incredible, from our, and any perspective.

– Very well, in order that you understand, let's begin, by explaining why you and I can get in touch, commented ÓMICRON by saying that; as I commented you previously, we have achieved that the velocity of light to become infinite, which enables, among many other things, that we may acquire information from any part of our universe and also from any point of any other parallel universe immediately.

This has allowed us to capture and know all the languages existent in any civilization, in any universe. On the other hand, our extremely powerful computers automatically translate our thoughts into messages that can understand the Daseins with which we get in touch, and that way we receive their respective messages in reciprocal form. Well, now I will proceed to cover some of the scientific and technological discoveries and inventions, that had achieved the civilizations level III, that you may understand, which additionally to everything that I have commented to you, are the following: the sense of hearing that they had preserved to be able to enjoy the wonder of music, was eliminated when they were able to perceive the intervening sound waves by their Daseins directly. That way, like all civilizations that happen in any universe, they invent gods, for whatever events they cannot explain themselves, in like manner, all civilizations invent, sooner or later music, activity for which we give priority importance.

At that point, Iturralde began to think about jazz, and immediately, he was in front of where all jazzmen that already had died were joined together, all were there, mentally chatting. He wondered: I would like to know what are they talking about, and immediately he received a cordial mental welcome, and they told him that they knew him perfectly well. He commented to them, that it was a true pity than in the Integritas no longer existed musical instruments, that he would have enjoyed to be able to listen to them playing. Their answer was, that it did not have the least importance, because here, they no longer need them anymore.

– What do you want to listen? Chet Baker asked Iturralde.

– Well here the magic continues Iturralde reflected; he forwarded the following request thought.

– I would like to listen a great big band, whose members are: Maynard Ferguson, Conrad Gozzo, Shorty Rogers, Carl Saunders …

– At that point Iturralde listened in his Dasein; Carl Saunders, has not died yet, he cannot participate now.

– That's right, I failed to see it, reflected Iturralde. And he kept on then, to complete the list of the musicians that he was wishing to listen to: Chet Baker and Clifford Brown, trumpets. Frank Rosolino, Jimmy Cleveland, Bill Russo, Carl Fontana and Bob Enevoldsen, trombones, Art Pepper, Paul Desmond, Bob Cooper, Bill Perkins and Pepper Adams, sax, Shelly Manne, drums, Scott La Faro, bass and Bob Florence, piano. And I would like to listen all that was recorded by all of you, on earth.

– Bob Florence asked Iturralde: do you want to listen, one by one, the melodies, or everything simultaneously, although you could listen to an immense number of melodies, you would listen each of them as you never listened to them on earth, and each of them without neither mixture nor interference of any kind, and besides, you will listen also all of our rehearsals, although they were not recorded (for sale, that is).

– Iturralde answers; Bob, thank you for the information, certainly I want to have this new experience of musical multiple reception.

What Iturralde listens then, is indescribable, really he is listening to 1,327 melodies simultaneously, with a beauty, perfection and acoustic quality, literally: *out of this world*. While enjoying that spectacular mixture, and at the same time, to the neat sound separation out of every melody, Iturralde listens to the voice of OMICRON, that tells him:

– You are able to listen boundlessly so much music and information, it is owed to the fact, that you received a very especial reward, due to your passion for music, but mainly because you never desired or practiced avarice, and also you never were envious. Actually, the one thing that you desired on earth, that may remotely be considered like envy, was to have wished to have musical and scientific talent, thus, I granted you an especial and eternal gift: the capability of joy, amplified to its maximum possible peak.

– Iturralde answers: thank you very much OMICRON, the gift that you have given me, is and will be, the cause of an unending and indescribable happiness for me.

While Iturralde found himself amazed with this musical, really spectacular joy, he thought about the rest of his family, the ones that had already died, when he realized that he had been thinking in several other matters and disregarded his family, placing them almost in last place. But strangely, he felt a sentiment of lack of priority, but he felt no other guilt whatsoever. And in that precise moment, he encountered himself in front of his grandparents, parents and brothers, what an overwhelming event!

He asked himself, will it exist here the musical pause? And at that moment, the musical reproduction ceased completely. That way, he dedicated himself to chat mentally with all of his family simultaneously, but he addressed himself to his father, in particular, to whom he did not know, while he was alive, given that his father, had died when Iturralde was only three months old. And that way, a shocking encounter was accomplished, between unknown father and unknown son.

The aforementioned mental conversation happens without sadness, but quite the contrary, they realize that the mentioned separation was only temporary. When meeting his father, Iturralde felt an indescribable joy. He asked him to chat about his life, which was a closed book to practically all of his father´s life. The history of the life of his father was told as follows; his father begins by telling that he had been born in Oaxaca, and he had become an orphan of father and mother when he was only six years old. One of his uncles adopted him, but he did not attend him like a son, but he employed him as his clerk. Instead of taking care of him, pampering him and sending him the school, he had him as a little boy employee, unsalaried, of course. The little boy wanted to progress, so he had his books under the counter, and in each opportunity that he found, he was reading, watching for the returning uncle, to hide the book, given the aggressive side of the uncle. This way, he got his basic education. His favorite subjects, and the ones that he was considering indispensable, were Spanish and Mathematics. Also, he learned English, that would be of great benefit, at a later time. When he became sixteen years old, he felt that he had sufficient preparation (and annoyed by the abusive uncle) he escaped to Mexico City. He was able to survive for a few years, and one fine day, he decided to establish his own business related to locks. It is here, where having learned English began to be of great utility. He managed to contact American lock manufacturers such as: Schlage and Corbin, those which rapidly named him a distributor in Mexico. At a later time talking with executives from the Johnson company – wax and machines to polish floors manufacturers –, equally named him a distributor. He continued getting distributions such as: Mosler safes and wooden floors. This happened in the Mexico of the twenties when a distribution got issued – by credibility on the word of a foreign businessman –, without resorting to lawyers, contracts in triplicate, or any other complications, or the distrust of our times. Also, at one time, he decided to manufacture milk for children, with the registered brand of – Choco Nutrina –, non-existent such powder milk in those years, which began to have instantaneous success. But unexpectedly, soon after he became ill and died, a little while later. Fortunately, as he started feeling weaker and sick every day, he trained his wife, who has to take, the not looked for responsibility to bring up, without the help of the father of six children, one of them only three months old, and the oldest only fourteen years old. Iturralde´s mother, with not much scholar education, that was the accustomed for the women in those times; six years of primary school and two additional of home-works, suddenly, she sees herself, from one day to the next, as a trader, in a men's world. Fortunately, the imperious need, her determination and her daily twelve hours of work, she manages not only to maintain the business, but to turn it into a prosperous and very well-known company, which was looked-for by the best engineers, architects and contractors of a Mexico in complete growth and with constructions of all types, by the hundreds. That way Iturralde and all of his brothers and sisters that wanted to study went to private schools. Iturralde thanks his parents and each of the family members embrace (mentally) each other with enormous happiness, and delighted to find each other again. Next Iturralde greets, with great affection, to his brother Fernando whom also he lost at premature age; – only twenty nine years old –, due to a heart attack. Iturralde is very grateful to him, since he was who showed Jazz to Iturralde. Iturralde commented that he missed him very much and that if he had lived, they could have had long Jazz sessions to listen to. The turn comes now to the rest of his family; grandparents and he had a good time chatting with his uncles, with whom he learned very much during his amenable and instructive conversations. In particular, he went to chat with his uncle Francisco who took care of him, he took him to various trips and he bought him a violin at an early age (which was not of his taste, so he studied it for a short time), but at a later time he bought him a trumpet, that Iturralde asked for, and this time he played it for several years.

For now on, they will be together for all eternity. Next Iturralde addressed his mother, with great love. He thanked her for all her affection and effort that she accomplished ta take care of the whole family, without the father. From his brother Fernando, he requests that he integrates with him and with all the musicians that were there, which he accepts gladly. Being now Iturralde in a family meeting, interchanging thoughts with each one and all members simultaneously, his musical passion that recently he has listened to, and a true high fidelity non-existent on earth, comes back to his mind, and automatically, and immediately he listens a voice that tells him, in his mind:

— Hi, I am Frank Rosolino, asking you, if you want to continue listening the same program, or if you want to change it, or to add more music. You can choose the musicians and the melodies that you want, without any restriction of any type and in any combination.

— Thanks Frank, answered Iturralde, for the moment, that way is fine and spectacular, I am going to go assimilating it, little by little, and in that precise moment, the return of the multiple concert that he had been listening continued.

Thinking about Chet Baker, Iturralde asked him:

— Without considering it in depth, Iturralde asked; could you teach me how to play trumpet? I dig your stile very much.

— Chet answered: unfortunately, what you did not learn on earth, your only opportunity to learn to play an instrument, no longer it be can learned here, remember that here, no longer exist any instruments.

Really, Chet is quite right. Also, no longer asking Bob Florence and Bill Holman for lessons on composition and arranging is appropriate, it is not possible to do it physically, however, mentally, it is possible.

Now Iturralde thinks about the musicians, and in addition to listening to the music and to chat with his family, he is chatting across with the musicians. Amazed now by the fact, that he is able to accomplish three activities simultaneously, he further thinks about other of the activities that impassioned him on earth, and that way, without interfering at all, he appeared in front of all of the professional and amateur Jai Alai players chatting heatedly on the most important games that they were remembering. Once more his amazement was increased, now Iturralde was able to see mentally, besides all of the parties already chatting, all the Jai Alai games that he ever watched. Apparently, the wonders here do not end, he told himself.

Well, we were not in heaven, but in Integritas purging our grief (very soft, indeed), before being able to enter *Agones*, or final destination prepared by Ómicron. Fine, if here where the beautiful gardens exceed imagination, and almost anything that anyone wants is fulfilled with only considering it. How much better the Agones must be? Because Integritas is much better than heaven, in *all respects*, all that happens, according to what is taught by the Catholic Church, is only to contemplate God, *for all eternity*, frankly what a bore.

Once satisfied that doubt, Iturralde returns to the conversation with…

– ÓMICRON whose explanation continues: our civilization has achieved an immense quantity of successful experiments of – parallel universes –, of which we took experience, to keep on obtaining even better results. And recently, that is, one hundred thousand million terrestrial years ago, in many of our experiments, we eliminated the inconvenient limit of the velocity of light. In said new universes, the velocity of light is infinite. Our technology permits us to employ infinite velocity of light, even when visiting universes that do not posses such updated feature.

– That takes care of, at least some of the validity of Einstein's Theory of Relativity, commented Iturralde, in relation to the limit of the velocity of light, that is amazing, and when I chat with Einstein, I will ask him his opinion, with regard to this matter.

– ÓMICRON made another comment: the sense of sight is the only one that we keep on preserving, but in a shape totally redesigned. Our eyes no longer deteriorate at all, and we are able to see, with perfect clarity, and without no additional accessories, from the smaller particles, like the quarks (than indeed exist, as your great scientist Stephen Hawking found out, that the smallest size of a particle of your universe has Planck's measured length of 1,61619 X 10^{-35} meters) to the outermost galaxies in any parallel universe, as well as each one of its integrating bodies, like galaxies, stars and planets, to all levels of approach. In this way, we converted evolution that achieved, without a designer, a good result for the eyes, – but extremely distant to a perfect design –, into a perfect visual instrument.

– How curious, manifested Iturralde, in one of my books, I mentioned that our eyes should have been provided with precisely that attribute, given that, according to the bible, god created the firmament for our delight, thus, if we are not capable of enjoying that marvelous view, it is an aberration.

– ÓMICRON continued: no doubt about it. In like manner, we are making experiments regarding static and dynamic universes, in relation to its expansion and or contraction. But, returning to the eyes issue, by the time we managed to make perfect eyes, our body counting on the few organs, that I commented to you, we had achieved a perfect health, because absolutely all diseases caused by parasites, bacteria and viruses were non-existent anymore, and all other diseases like diabetes, heart attacks, cancer and the rest, had been eliminated completely. We achieved this, when finally we could find all the genes that produce aging, as well as any diseases, so that way we managed to maintain our bodies with indefinite life. In like manner, we redefined our principal life parameters, such as the temperature of our bodies by the transference of genes of plants, in order to be able to bear light and solar heat all day long, every day, as well as, very heavy rain that could not affect us, at all. From animals, similar to your polar bears and penguins, we took genes that allowed us to bear temperatures of 100 degrees centigrade, below zero. Also, from bacteria that live near the hot marine chimneys, we took the genes that allows them to lead a decent life, in excess of 100 degrees centigrade. Even more, the aforementioned genes were modified and upgraded, in such a way, that now we can tolerate much more extreme temperatures in the thermic range.

Then, we finally achieved the great feat of eliminating the aging process, this does not mean that death is inexistent, eventually, due to some accident. But, nevertheless, this does not prove to be so serious, like in the past. Now, given that we keep the complete genetic information of all the inhabitants of our civilization, in the aforementioned situation, which occurs, very unfrequently, then we immediately proceeded to cloning and given that all the mental information of each individual is kept, as I explained to you previously, it is send to his/her corresponding Dasein, in such a form that said individual that has died, will go back to life, having the exactly same personality that he/her was having previously. That, in fact, practically makes us to have everlasting life.

– ÓMICRON keeps on: You had already the opportunity to experience the advance of our *telepathy* which is like an unlimited wideband as to the number of channels, which allows all the Daseins to be communicated in simultaneous form, without the least interference, each Dasein has unlimited channels of simultaneous reception, which you have been experiencing and enjoying since your arrival to this place. Our previous civilization; level II, saw the need to turn to eugenics process, in order to be able to, count on perfect beings that they could enable our civilizations' progress. It is totally evident that Darwinian evolution, by itself, given that has no specific purpose in mind, each improvement delays a long time, and the produced changes, are not the best possible results.

– I see the point, Iturralde commented, in my time that was not allowed (but most surely, it was done). My point of view agrees with this technique, since it seems to be the one and only process that provokes the changes that you are interested in achieving.

– In that way we proceeded to a similar reproduction procedure that you utilized when modifying dogs' races, with the purpose of achieving increasingly better races in all respects. We proceeded to cloning our best specimens and we went back, repeatedly, to choose the more apt, learned, prepared, intelligent and wise persons, and only in that form, we managed to improve our civilization's levels, to catch up with our present-day level IV. We have produced beings with perfect intelligence in that form, ineffectual of the least thought of wrongdoing. The aforementioned minds, which are perfect computers, only attempt to increase even more their knowledge, to enjoy music and many other activities of intellect and being happy. As previously commented, something that was vital to attain in our development, was the total disappearance of money that causes avarice, which corrupts everything.

This was feasible, once that it was possible for us, not to need to feed ourselves with food. Once the climate no longer affected us at all, the need for a house no longer was necessary. Finally, we returned to live very close to nature, of which we are an unseparable part. It took several advances of civilizations levels to understand, how ironical! And given that all our robots accomplished all kinds of necessary work, getting energy directly from the stars and galaxies, and we no longer were in any need of getting energy from any type for our body, we could get rid of the cursing of money. In our present time, absolutely all required work is accomplished by automatic and intelligent robots that obey every order that we give them, by the mere fact that any one of us think in the order, that we want to be accomplished. All robots that exist are made, in like manner, by robots without the need of any intervention from our part. In the very remote situation, that becomes necessary a new type of robot, our robotic machinery design and manufacture in a totally automatic way a new robot perfectly designed by our designer robots.

– How interesting ÓMICRON, given that you commented concepts that were know in earth, everything seems very comprehensible to me, Iturralde comments back. What can you tell me now with respect to the force of gravity?

– Well replies ÓMICRON, in relation to that important and interesting point, once we found that gravitons really exist, like bosons particles that transmit the gravitational interaction of Quantic Gravity.

JOSÉ OCTAVIO VELASCO-TEJEDA

We found that way, eons back, that the String Theory is correct. And now we can modify the force of gravity to our convenience, which allows us the modification of the atoms of galaxies, black holes and even complete universes.

– Very interesting comments Iturralde, what can you tell me about your means of travel?

– Our journeys can be local, that is, to any place within our galaxy, or else to any of the parallel existent universes, by means of extremely quick worm's holes.

– How do you make good use of your work time, and regarding your free and leisure time?

– Regarding work, just as I let you know before, does no longer exist in our civilization. Everything is executed perfectly by robots, when it becomes necessary, the most that we have to do, is to tell a robot whatever is needed to perform, and the robot entrusts the accomplishing of the task with 100% of accuracy and rapidity. But, if you guess than we get bored, at any time, you are mistaken, the majority of our intellectual activities, including our games, are not understandable by you, at this moment. But, what I can tell you with pleasure is that, we imitated your civilization's chess game, which is the only one worthwhile for us, due to the necessity to utilize the intelligence, because luck does not intervene at all. That game is very popular in our civilization. Tournaments become organized frequently, and like I mentioned it to you before, our only reward is the *internal* satisfaction to have intellectually defeated to one of our peers. Never there are fighting arguments or envies. We are civilized, – in all the extension of the word –. Period. In like manner, a very popular activity is to observe galaxies in various parallel universes, you can imagine that we are kept very busy just exploring them, and later in the *work* in the formation of unending catalogs to classify them, if keeps us occupied for quite a while, but we enjoyed it very much. Another very common activity is to listen music, but as indicated to you, as well as, verified by yourself, we can accomplish all activities in simultaneous form, remaining concentrated in total form, in everything, and each of the realized activities. The concepts concerning; *absent-minded,*

I forgot, I did not realize it, are not applicable for us. Regarding to rest; an hour each year, is the recommended relax time, referring to a terrestrial equivalent.

– Iturralde, more and more amazed, asks the following; the question regarding if mathematics are a human invention, or if they exist independently of our mind, has existed during centuries on earth, what is your answer?

– I am going to answer you by means of an analogy; when a tree falls in an inhabited jungle, without some human or animal present to hear the noise, the aforementioned noise does exists or does not exist? Evidently, the noise exists independently to if it is heard by some animal or not. In similar form, mathematics exist independently of any civilization discovering them or not. And its branches are infinite as well as the numbers. It is for this reason that your civilization is constantly discovering new mathematical areas, for which applications appear, and many others that apparently belong to pure mathematics, and however time after they appear, – like a ring to a finger –, to be used in practical form. An example of this situation was Riemann's space geometry, which was used by Einstein for his Theory of Relativity. However, we know that in everything civilizations which evolves, that gets to the point of developing intelligence, any type of genetics or its equivalent contains a mathematical predecessor, that is, an innate tendency to go discovering the wonders of mathematics progressively.

I assure you, with all certainty, that without mathematics (and later other branches of science), no advanced civilizations exist. Unfortunately, science, badly utilized, as in your instance, almost with certainty, that kind of civilization inevitable self-destructs itself, when they discover the atomic energy. For the time being, I no longer can continue commenting to you, regarding our advances, any of them would be unintelligible for your understanding, at all.

– All right ÓMICRON, thank you very much, for so much and important information, that you have provided me with.

Now Iturralde remembers his work on earth, that was so important and interesting, given that involved utilizing the mind to solve problems of any type, especially at the start of the era of computer programming; the interesting computer IBM 1401, the first commercial model, and, at a later time, the series 360, 370, 3031 and 3033. Also he was attracted immensely to system analysis like, for example, the payroll that was designed and implemented for one of the companies that he worked for. I want to meet Tom Watson senior and his son of same name, the IBM's founder and great impact innovator, respectively. Immediately both solicited personages appeared before Iturralde and began chatting regarding the fabulous benefits that their company provided for its employees, during a good part of the long period when Iturralde was himself one of them. Iturralde, who was a fervent and loyal worker for said enterprise, told the former owners, about the nasty experiences that the newer CEO, and other high level managers, purposely damaged him regarding his career therein, to the point of literally forcing him to resign, and also he did not received a very significant bonus (about the salary corresponding to four years of labor), due to an anticipated retirement plan, for every wishing employee, that had been working during, at least fifteen years, which he had, when he left the company. As a result, he detested the company that he had appreciated years before. The Watsons commented to Iturralde that, in fact, their company had changed its policies dramatically, and that they were very sorry, regarding said behavior, and that if any of them had been alive, and in function, at that specific instance, that would had not happened. Iturralde was glad to hear this, because he had great admiration for these two capable personages. At that point, Iturralde could observe also John Napier, the inventor of the wonderful Slide Rule, indispensable for the engineers for decades, to Blaise Pascal and his calculator Pascalina invention, to Gottfried Leibniz designer and constructor of another calculator, and to Sir Isaac Newton's, writer of the indispensable book: *Principia Mathematica*, which contains so much information about quite a few physic disciplines, without forgetting that he, and independently, Gottfried Leibniz, discovered the absolutely indispensable Calculus. Also, Charles Babagge, the designer of the Differential Machine, which can be considered as the first computer ever, that had a memory, where it could store variables, constants and results obtained and printed in paper. Said machine was controlled by a sequence of instructions (a program) and had input-output units, which already contained all the fundamental bases that constitute a modern computer. Also Babagge recognized Herman Hollerith who utilized punch cards to manufacture a tabulating machine than he himself utilized in the poll of 1890 in the U.S. Within view were, Prespert Eckert and John Mauchly that designed and implemented the giant-sized ENIAC and after they founded the UNIVAC company. Alongside was John Von Newman, who was considered as the father of modern computers, who in turn, also supervised Alan Touring's doctoral dissertation, and who constructed a formal model of the so-called, Touring's computer machine and who also proved that there were such problems that a machine could not solve. Next to him, Norbert Wiener who among other things; coined the term cybernetic, so utilized with respect to the computers.

A very curious situation, that Iturralde came to understand, was that with only looking the face of a Dasein, immediately he had exact notion to whom he was viewing, even when he had not known the person when they were alive, thus, he was observing; John Bardeen, Walter Brattain and William Shockley the transistor inventors, without which, the invention of modern computers could not possibly had happen. Well, like in all the other situations in which by only thinking in a theme, there appeared before him automatically, absolutely everybody implicated in that related field, in this occasion, also multitudes of scientists and engineers related with the computers, were joined together. Iturralde thought, here, what is in surplus, is time, so later on, I will like to chat, with each of these so interesting people, creators of wonders (he was supposed to have thought about Daseins, not people), although they only had importance in the terrestrial time and space. From now on, for a while, the scientists were next in line, given that Iturralde´s thought, in the branch of culture that was so much of his interest on earth. So much, that science was the contents of most of the books that he was basically reading, most of the time. And he thought, more or less chronologically in proceeding to know each person, that is, (in spirit), the great Greek originators of science, that Iturralde remembered perfectly well, the more important contributions that had been achieved by each "giant", in this and in all the other important areas that were interesting for him while he was alive. Iturralde found Archimedes in front of his line of sight, considered for many scientists as the greatest of them of all of times, in spite of the not much information regarding his work, which was recovered in a palimpsest, where his invaluable work was overwritten with prayers (how *funny* monks). Iturralde commented to the inventor that; the aforementioned palimpsest revealed, once it was reconstructed by means of several very complicated and delayed technologies, such as: conservation, image-ology, and utilization of the Livermore's synchrotron, the amazing diversity of practical knowledge there encountered, such as; the invention of the lever, the screw, the principle of floatability, weapons of defense (utilized by his city is Syracuse against the Romans) like the catapults and concentrators lenses that reflected heat to burn ships. And in the theoretic aspect, amazing feats such as; the calculation of the center of gravity of triangles and another figures, and nothing less that; the differential and integral calculus, over two millennia before Sir Isaac Newton discover it, and in independent form Gottfried Leibniz. Had that invention been utilized in that ancient epoch, civilization would have begun to advance two millennia earlier. Archimedes was very happy to learn the way that his lifetime work had become known, rather late, but nonetheless important. At a later time Iturralde would return with him, because there was very much to learn from him and to know his experiences.

Next, Iturralde could see Pythagoras; any little boy attending primary school learns the formula $C^2 = A^2 + B^2$ (the square of the hypotenuse is equal to the sum of the squares of the sides of a triangle for all right-angled triangles) theorem which was discovered and proved true by him and that carries his name. Pythagoras and his school affirmed that everything is a number, so they dedicated to study and classify numbers. Given that Pythagoras was one of the first scientists studying the musical scale and understanding the relation of the length of a string that vibrates with the notes produced by it. There is established again, than in music also, a number is everything. Music was Iturralde's passion, thus, here was another scientist, with whom he could go several millennia chatting with him. In the meantime, Iturralde thank Pythagoras for all his contributions regarding music and science.

Iturralde detected Fermat, and being face to face with him, mentioned his last theorem, which refers, in turn to, Pythagoras's theorem, but where Fermat declares emphatically, that this formula *only* is valid for power 2, that is; equation $C^3 = A^3 + B^3$ does not provides an exact solution, (also with any other larger power). In other words; such a very simple equation, that a little boy attending primary school can understand, had not gotten solved during over three hundred and fifty years, by the greatest mathematicians that lived in the cited centuries, not to be able to demonstrate it, mathematically. The originator of the aforementioned, so called; *last Fermat theorem.* Pierre Fermat, wrote a little note on one of his books relating that he had already worked the required proof, but that there was not enough space for writing the complete proof, in the margin of said book.

– Iturralde asked Fermat about this enigma.

– Fermat´s answer was a smile.

The notable mathematician that finally solved the enigma; Andrew Wiles. He required to combine various mathematical theories and even a conjecture (a non-demonstrated hypothesis). That mathematical demonstration was contained in *two-hundred sheets.* Even so, when first presented to his colleagues in Cambridge, which got surprised with that quite amazing feat. However; any hypothesis, theory or mathematical demonstration, when presented itself officially, is submitted to exhaustive revision by peers, where they try, by all means available, to find the least fault, in order to discard said document, or else, if absolutely all what's been shown is presented in an impeccable form, it is accepted like something certain. With regard to the once successful theories related to physics, with certain frequency, the theories present, small or great incongruences that are revised by a posterior theory, which replaces the previous one; an accepted procedure that permits that advancement of science. With relation regarding a *mathematical demonstration,* however, once accepted is considered true forever. It is for this reason that said revisions of mathematical demonstrations are so demanding and revised, to complete detail, by several expert mathematicians in each area. While observing Pierre Fermat, Iturralde asked him, if he did really had demonstrated his own theorem, with the existent mathematics in his epoch. Fermat answered, this time in a serious mood; no, unfortunately I have to recognize that I failed to complete the proof, I must of have committed a basic error that did not detect then, now I give myself account that Wiles managed to accomplish it, utilizing mathematical areas, completely unknown to me. Now, Fermat and all the other great mathematicians, that failed the great challenge, commented the astonishing mathematical capabilities of Wiles.

– Iturralde asks now, ÓMICRON please answer this other question; I find myself in the equivalent of paradise, but given that I did not believe in god, – and even worse–, I had written a book, "demonstrating", his non-existence, so what is the truth?

– ÓMICRON answered that it was false that unbelievers, would be condemned, if they had behaved properly on earth, and that they would be able to go to Integritas, independently of if they professed any religion or if they had faith in ÓMICRON's existence (god's equivalent), or even if they were agnostics, or even worse: atheists. So faith spread out and was accepted on earth, it was a human invention, an invention of all the different religions for controlling *humans,* which do not want to accept the proofs provided by science. ÓMICRON does not need anyone to believe in him, let alone that they be praying to him continuously in all the planet, given that he cannot intervene in any situation. I will explain to you how, why and for what reason, does the earth exists.

Respect to how; the universe itself was formed by means of the Big Bang, as correctly the terrestrial scientists propose it. ÓMICRON's only intervention in this process, that at a later time will form all the galaxies, planets and all other heavenly bodies, was to adjust the physical constants, in order that the cosmos be formed. Said constants; very well calculated by myself, contain the following values: the enormous N number; $- 10^{36} -$, the ratio of the strengths of gravity to that of electromagnetism in relation to gravity and the cosmos measure the electric power that maintain the atoms united. Stars, the periodic table and atoms depend on the value; $- 0.007 -$ the strength of the force binding nucleons to the nuclei of the atoms. The constant D has the value; $- 3 -$, and stands for the number of dimensions. In similar form, I decide about the rest of the necessary values of the cosmic parameters, so the cosmos may be functional. ÓMICRON is quite satisfied with this universe, with a very important exception;

humans, who were very lucky given that evolution endow them with a very complicated and a capable brain of great actions, not only for the creation of civilization, but for something tremendously important, that it is, the adequate utilization of said great brain, in order that they construct civilizations that work in accord with nature and with his fellowmen.

It is completely false that god assigned man to; "dominate nature and to abuse and waste all of what's existent on earth, for him only". All animals and plants have exactly the same right to live and to be treated with benevolence. Unfortunately, evolution, by itself, implies for living animals to eat themselves to survive, but this is supposed to be treated with the maximum care; only killing to eat, without cruelty, without waste and without excess. For simple common sense, let alone intelligence, humans not yet have become aware of the damage that they have caused to the planet, and that way, right now, they have deranged all of the united ecological complex, which if not react globally, hurriedly and rationally they are in extreme danger to cause damages, that in all probability, no longer will be reversible. And since I am talking to you with reference to the human being, it is also absolutely false, of course, that man has something to do, in relation to ÓMICRON's image, they have not found out, and he has not yet given credit to Darwin, for the brilliant discovery of the concept of evolution, where clearly is totally verifiable, that man is an ape, the chimpanzee's first closest cousin. This comparison of invented descent clearly could be offensive to practically any superior being, however, that ridicule assumption does not cause the least inconvenience to ÓMICRON. It is just completely out of place.

You, humans, had the incredible luck that your universe was formed with said adjusted constants that would enable, millions of years after, the formation of earth, where with its so especial characteristics, would enable the evolution of life until all animals arose and finally humans. Additionally, when in any planet, once evolution was started with intelligent animals, ÓMICRON intervenes to endow them with Daseins (when dying, like right now, with yourself, which I indicated to you previously), where, if they utilized their brain intelligently, they would receive a reward of eternal life, and otherwise eternal punishment.

In relation to the *why;* Outside of these *small* interventions, ÓMICRON does not want to intervene in the worldly functioning, because humans are accomplishing an extremely important experiment for me. In like manner, in the other parallel universes that exist, ÓMICRON modifies slightly the adjustment of the physical constants to see what results, millions of years after, not intervening again, in the least. Being ÓMICRON the greatest architect, mathematician, and scientist that exists, literally anywhere, I practice large-scale experimentation, having my more important priorities; to achieve designing universes, with the only interventions that I mentioned to you previously, and that fulfill all of the characteristics desired.

With respect to: *the reason why the earth exists*: ÓMICRON is fare and he is interested that humans behave in like manner on earth and to help to each other. For ÓMICRON, one of the most punishable attitudes is avarice. This must be that way, since in that planet the human being evolved, who was provided with a prodigious brain, which, generally is utilized very poorly, this waste and wrongdoing is punished, as well as good behavior is rewarded.

These answers provided Iturralde an enormous satisfaction, every person (or Dasein) likes to be right. That confirmation proved Iturralde that his books, were correct. Mainly, because they had been verified by ÓMICRON. That way, it was clear that, all religions had been created by men with the only attempt to deceive the people for their own benefice and acquiring power to control the faithful.

ÓMICRON, on purpose, has not given proof of his existence, because he does not want that within his experiments exist factors that may alter somehow the results. ÓMICRON wants that, when evolution produce intelligence, of a certain level, intelligent animals, without any hint whatsoever that they may later could receive a reward or punishment, utilize their intelligence, by own conviction, to live together adequately with their family, as well as, with the rest of their fellow neighbors around the planet, and with the planet itself. The fact that ÓMICRON only adjusts the physical constants with reference to each parallel universe, he prepares the specific *tomos* (punctual and divisible, not the atoms, – name incorrectly utilized –) for each parallel universe, which will produce the correspondent Big Bang, when ÓMICRON *disappears*, without making clear proof of his existence.

In that way Iturralde, finds himself in Integritas, where ÓMICRON, who has under his command, an army of helpers, whose task is ask to millions of proto-Daseins (pre-souls) if they want to be born, that is, to inhabit a human body, or the one belonging to some other intelligent animal, in some other planet. In this mental proto-Dasein, they can observe the planet where they would be born, as well as, which country. They will be able to make a choice also, regarding sex, skin texture, and some other physical characteristics. Religion is going to depend on the country chosen, in this aspect, Ómicron, respects the religion chosen, simply because, that is the way it exist at that place. He knows them absurd and human made, but he can do nothing with regard to this matter. In like manner, there are shown the terrible problems that earth (or any other chosen planet) may be facing during his/her lifetime, and for the two later generations (in this stage a more limited vision of the future exists). In that way, the proto-Dasein will be able to decide what option chooses. That is, it represent the option; do you want to live? or pass?

For the proto-Dasein that decides not to be born (to have a body on a planet) and that therefore he/she will not experience terrestrial life, there are provided oceans of additional options (another planets in various universes). These proto-Daseins, must search and find a planet in the same galaxy where they are, or else, by entering a *worm's tunnel,* to travel to another parallel universe, and there look for some inhabitable planet, that attracts them for living there. But definitively, if they do not find a birthplace, the proto-Dasein will be some errant proto-Dasein from universe to universe.

Iturralde learning about this earth-shattering option, does not remember, in the least, that he had the aforementioned option, more than likely, he reasons, once you were born, you no longer remember it, like all what happens during the baby stage, however, he felt enormously lucky from having been born *exactly with all the characteristics that he received*, which gives him a lot of pleasure. He reflects: if the least detail would have changed, with great probability, all that he loved in his whole life had not proven to be the same. That way, all the desirable events that occurred to him in his life, that is, exactly the way I would have chosen to be born. There were myriads of events out of his control, but even so, he loved that life, at least, for the part regarding my family, environment and my tastes. But, most probably, there were multitude of happenings that definitively were not in accord, before being born, because they had not been consulted, for example; epoch of birth, country, relatives, etc.

– I have a question Ómicron: if each proto-Dasein can make a choice of so many possible options, why we find so many poor, uneducated people, how was it possible that they had made so bad a choice?

– Iturralde, if you remember, of the several options to make a choice, it was never mentioned, the social standing, because this is going to depend on the parents that happen to be specified for that particular proto-Dasein, those who not even myself know who they will be. This *proto-soul-landing* proceeds in sequential form. There exists a proto-Dasein queue that is going to go occupying the bodies of the babies that will be born in strict birth date and time. Good and bad luck are what decides which parents will be their relatives. Given that there exist a greater proportion of parents of low social standing, than the ones that exist with good social standing, it is what accounts for the situation that you asked me. No, they did not make a bad choice, they had bad luck. That is the main reason that stops irresolute proto–Dasein from taking a decision to be born, because they expect a situation, at least with better odds, but that we cannot guarantee to them. Therefore, remembering some games where a player is asked if he will take a card, or not; the dealer says: *do you want to play (take a card)? or pass*, it is from there, where we took the question that we ask them.

You will remember, Iturralde, that I mentioned before that the bigger problem that we were deeming to resolve was the relating to entropy, that as you know, it is the constant increase of disorder. So you can have additional knowledge, I want to tell you, that I have just been informed, that we already have sufficient and convincing information, that in one of our parallel universes entropy has been stamped out. What does this mean? That starting right now, from now on, all new universe that we unroll will be eternal. No longer aging or deterioration will exist, either for matter alive or inert. Of course this enormous achievement will call for very important changes in a great various segments deals, as are the following:

Dust no longer will exist in the enormous clouds that form the galaxies, they will be designed with said new form of technology; the matter that replaces it, is not dirty and has a lot more cohesion, in other words: it will be harder to crumble down, and will be much heavier. This will be due, to the much less empty space that form each *tome* (remember, that it is the real name for the prior atom), which encompasses, more matter and less empty space.

All; star, planet, meteorite, quasar, red giant, neutron star and black hole, will have instruments that will impede any collision, allowing, for the first time in the history of the universes, that beautiful bodies get destroyed, and also the fact that, in so repeated occasions, they have caused the almost total extermination of all the sorts of living creatures. This is, really, a well-designed universe. No longer Super-Novas, Red Giants, Gamma Rays, or Cosmic Rays will exist, which are so destructive to even very distant bodies, because we want to avoid such damage and destruction.

For those who want to travel to another place of the galaxy, within the same universe, the wormholes prove to be very adequate, comfortable and fast (to the velocity of light). In the event of desiring to travel to a parallel universe, there exist instant roads, that is, especial worms' holes (without the bordering of the velocity of light).

Meanwhile, evolution will keep on; as the *designer* of all sort of living things that may appear, with the same previous bases, that is, the survival of the fittest. However, we have included some variants in this new universe, foodstuff will not be necessary any longer, thus predators will not exist. These new animals, will get its energy from the sun, exactly like we do, and from its birth, they will have a bigger capability of intelligence, permitting that during their lifetime, they may increment it with bigger amplitude and rapidity. Also I made a comment to you previously that, until we find a solution to the problem of entropy, all our places where we inhabit, as well as your planet's Daseins and other ones inhabited, they would remain there, but when we find the definite sought-after solution for it, or even a less substantial improvement, which we already have found, all of the above will be re-localized in that enhanced universe, which will proceed in consequence, in the near future. This great achievement, is due to the fact that, mathematics are infinite in all of its branches. We are in constant learning, and in search of new branches, which prove to be pure mathematics, that is, without practical apparent utility, but sometime after, requests appear that enable us to utilize them. It was due to this effort that I comment to you, which allowed us, at last, to find such sensational discovery. Our civilization, like the terrestrial, continue basing all its scientific and technological development in mathematical models, which, they indicate us, with almost all certainty, what works and what not. Very important! I indicated to you, that the limit to the velocity of light, no longer existed for us, in certain circumstances. It was in this new universe, where this earth-shattering event was achieved. It is sad that Einstein's merit was surpassed, but that is the way science works, never there is definite or final learning, always advance, over and over again. Also, we increased the velocity of sound to one hundred kilometers per second on average, depending on the factors that modify it, according to the universe where it operates. For the time being, this new velocity, seems sufficiently convenient to us. I have not told you about our absolute control of gravity. Imagine a variable light control, utilized in a modern lamp from earth. In similar form we can control the gravity in any area, in any way it is desired or needed. Not only to have gravity, or not, we can graduate it according to our needs or desires. This *appliance* is especially useful for us, when visiting a dwarf white star or a neutron star, where they present very powerful gravitational fields.

Additionally, continued Ómicron: In order to achieve a bigger variety of universes, we not only modified the basic constants, we have also modified the design of the basic atom that you know. Indeed Democritus had a precise intuition of how all matter is formed. One of the new *tomes* that is working very encouragingly consists in two nuclei, that is, similar to a system of binary stars, but miniature. Given that the greater part of the mass of a *tome* is concentrated in its nucleus, if its mass duplicates, evidently the weigh gets doubled, which allows achieving unthinkable things, like the one that I described to you, about entropy. We are accomplishing several other experiments, like the one referring to the following; increasing the mass of the electron, of the proton and of the neutron. One by one, and in every combination. In like manner; reducing or increasing the size of the orbits of the electrons shows that we can obtain new properties. With certainty, we will find situations not even dreamt of, that they will provide us with practical applications in our civilization. To the possibility of known different possible universes; with a design of more heavy *tomes,* the variety of possible universes grows substantially. Therefore; *now we have new investigations for a long while*, as you would say on earth. Talking about new universes, the way to create them, continues to be the known Big Bang, which, you can imagine, is the most dangerous event that exists. All precautions may be insufficient. The least oversight could destroy the universe in which the testing of a new universe is being prepared or implemented. Therefore, parallel universes, exclusively for testing of new universes exists. Needless to mention that all of the preparations are implemented by intelligent robots, which manipulate the new parallel *baby* universe, a punctual element, which once triggered, it will produce thousands of million degrees centigrade of temperature and an expansion and fast growth of the new universe (which your great scientist, Allan Guth, called *inflation*). That universe for testing is of scarce magnitude, and becomes useless for other utilization. As determined by your scientist Einstein, the universe, as it spreads out, creates its own space time.

– Ómicron continues: It am afraid that I can no longer provide you with more information, regarding the advanced civilizations, because it would be unintelligible to you. Certainly anyone who finds himself in Integritas in permanent form, and besides he/she is interested, will be able to begin to learn said interesting information. What I have transmitted to you, is the equivalent to what a little boy in his first year of primary school on earth will learn, as compared, with what a scientist with several doctorates has learned, in order that you give yourself an idea, of the level of information that you have just learned, and the one that is still missing.

– Yes, definitely, Iturralde answers, I can't imagine any further thought, even trying to apply all the new knowledge that you gently chatted with me.

ÓMICRON is unable to see the future (beyond two terrestrial centuries), and he cannot, at all, know the future, regarding evolution. What ÓMICRON can do, is to select the constants that prove to be more favorable for the parallel universes in all aspects, especially in the one related to the continuous improvement of intelligence.

It may exist a civilization level V, which not even Ómicron can imagine, Iturralde reflects.

Iturralde, for scarce minutes had clinical death, he managed to travel through a worm's tunnel and lived an experience in another dimension, however, the doctors are trying to rescue him from death. In the aforementioned particular situations, applies the option: to *return to life or pass*. It is relatively simple for this so advanced civilization to *click* the option: return to life. The procedure consists in reopening the specific worm's tunnel where Iturralde got himself to the Integritas. When doing this, the Dasein that passed through, returns to earth and back to life, in the body from where it left. That way, the last contact with ÓMICRON happens, when he directly asks Iturralde;

– Do you want to live? or pass

Iturralde, taking into account the good life, that he had the luck to live, answers almost immediately;

– I want to live! After all, I right now know the great life that I can expect after my death on earth, and given that, it will be forever, and that life on earth, is lived only once, I want to have a good time with my family, for some more years in my planet: thank you very much Ómicron.

– Your decision seems excellent to me, ÓMICRON answers, I want to give you a gift, an indisputable proof that really you lived this experience. This proof is not constituted on one part, but rather in two parts. The first part is to reveal to you, the exact date and place where Steve Jobs is going to die, due to cancer: October 5 of 2011, in Palo Alto, California. Who, by that time, will have presented, with enormous success; the presentations of the Ipod, the Ipad, and of the Iphone. The second part is that; on July 4, 2012, CERN will announce the discovery and proof of the existence of the Higgs's boson at said laboratory. Memorize these data well, they are very important.

Also, I want you to know something else, that will give you a great deal of pleasure, I congratulate you for all the passions that you had on earth, all of them of great intellectual value. Also, that I like very much the classical music and principally Jazz, – your civilization's great invention –, I listen to it all the time. Our advanced civilizations may have invented and produced big wonders, but we could not found some musical genre that proved to be better than Jazz, in particular; its variety of rhythms, the so intelligent, happy and pleasant way to utilize European harmony and counterpoint, and of course, something that proves to be better than improvisation does not exist. Neither in your civilization, nor in any other one. This great art we could not have accomplished, for the simple reason, that we could never neither count with the instruments that you invented, nor for utilized material – brass –, but mainly, because the shape of our body does not lend itself, to be able to play such wonders. I am commenting to you again this issue, because we consider it of great importance.

– ÓMICRON, thank you for everything, it was a pleasure knowing you (even it was only by means of telepathy) and chatting with you, and what amount of information, about advanced civilizations you were pleased to share to me. I will contact you later, Iturralde thanked repeatedly. Pardon my insolence, I do not want to seem uneducated or something like that to you, but may I consider myself, your friend?

– Of course, I am pleased that you ask me, the great little chat that we had, proved that it is a reality, count on that.

When Iturralde wakes up, at the surgery ward, and the doctor comments to him, that he can relax very peacefully, that the surgical procedure was successful, thus, he tries to find out, if everything was a dream (was it?). That leaves him pensive because, if ÓMICRON exists, for Iturralde, the situation of the births, where each creature, before being born has options to make a choice that can decide about his future, at least relative to his start. At that point his wife gives him a kiss and holds his hand. Iturralde comments her that he had an incredible dream, and that it could be worth to write a book about this dream. Perhaps, someday, he will write that book, when he has some free time. It was some kind of a dream, which he remembered the happenings apparently quite real, with so many details and so much lasting that, Iturralde frequently asked himself if it was only a dream, or he already had the opportunity to travel to another dimension. Having Iturralde scientific bases, he was skeptical by nature, but he had personal indications of a possibility of an afterlife, but he never will be able to know, in this world, the reality of what he lived, he thought or he dreamt.

As soon as the effects of the anesthesia ceased and he recovered his consciousness totally, he asked for a pen and paper to one of the nurses, and he wrote, what he remembered regarding what ÓMICRON had commented to him. He told to himself: if I write all that I remember of all my dreams, I'll be wasting time miserably, given that the majority of dreams and nightmares are absurd and impossible or annoying. But this dream was so real that, in order not to quit, I am going to make a note of it. Back in his house, seeing than the deadlines in the paper, referred to a later decade, he took the note to his office, and dropped it, in an envelope that contained memories of journeys and trips; airplane tickets, hotel reservations, etc. Since this had been another journey (dreamt, at least), according to the passing of time, he went away forgetting that business completely, such complication of health, from which he recovered, to a considerable extent, and of all its related matters.

In a certain occasion, approximately a decade later from his surgery, during a family gathering, Iturralde's cousin, who was the only one case within his family, in becoming the proud possessor of a diploma as a master's in physics at the MIT and also a Ph. D, at the Max Planck Institute in Germany, and therefore keenly aware of everything that happened in the sphere of science, and knowing that also Iturralde was interested,

– He comments to Iturralde: are you aware, that they already find Higgs's boson at the CERN laboratory?

– No, not at all, please tell me details, answered Iturralde.

That way, his cousin told Iturralde a certain amount of the referred issue, unknown to him, given that Iturralde does not like to read newspapers, or to listen news bulletins, let alone watching television.

Coming out of that meeting, although it was a holiday, Iturralde addressed himself to his office, remembering vaguely the information that presumably ÓMICRON had provided him. He had referred to something about a very important cosmic or nuclear discovery, that is: infinitely big or small. Did he chatted with me about a super-nova or some black hole? No, definitively, not! It was related to something pertaining to a discovery at nuclear level, and something that scientists have been on the lookout, for a very long time. I kind of remember that Ómicron referred to the Higgs's boson. For that reason, something clicked in the memory, when his cousin mentioned that important discovery.

Right now, at least one of predictions, so difficult to realize, unless his memory was failing, had taken place, it was absolutely imperious for him, to read the written information, and checking if coincidence in the details existed. Already in his automobile, he desired to arrive at his office very rapidly, even by exciding the speed limits, and without respecting traffic lights, but he remembered Napoleon´s quote, that he told to his servants, when they were dressing him, with his solemn uniform, to command an important battle: "Get things done slowly, because I am in a hurry". And in this way, he drove as quickly as possible, but without causing any transit rule braking, that may cause a delay. Finally, he arrived to his office, he opened the door and run up the stairs, in order to look for the envelope keeper of memories of tours, where he had kept the paper written in the hospital, close to ten years back.

He found the envelope immediately, since he was very orderly, he took a seat in his armchair, and opened it with shaky and sweaty hands and his heart yapping, as if running a marathon. He delayed a little bit in finding the possible certificate, more valid than a notary public document, from the other dimension. With the paper in hand, he turned on his computer and looked searching for the Higgs's boson web pages. Immediately several pages appeared on the screen with regard to this matter. He opened the one that appeared more revealing to him, and there he found all of the concurring data that was appearing within his hospital written note.

Iturralde did not fit himself with amazement. Getting back his breath, as if the marathon would really had ended, and now more relaxed, he thought: my goodness: what a fantastic coincidence. Now, let's see what I score, in relation to the other prediction. He no longer had memory that this referred to Steve Jobs himself. When reading it, he remembered that he had found out about his death, but he had not related it to his note. So, immediately he look for any page in the Internet that referred to that notable character, a brilliant brain, provoking mind-bogging inventions. Iturralde found: Steven Paul Jobs (San Francisco, California, February 24, 1955, Palo Alto, California, October 5, 2011)

It was good fortune, that Iturralde found himself seated. He received a brutal impact, he was completely shocked. He felt a mixture of amazement, joy and gratitude that he never had experienced, and in all likelihood, never would happen again. He went back to reread the note, by far more slowly and careful, when he noticed a patterned seal that was covering part of what he had written. The seal read: "HOSPITAL ANGELES DEL PEDREGAL" and it could be read, with enough sharpness in the bottom part: April 3 2002 and 11:07. He now remembered the event neatly. For medical recommendation, his initial angioplasty's recuperation consisted in small walks, within the hospital, for which, in order to take the opportunity to know the hospital, Iturralde, changed his route in every occasion. During a new route, he went by the one side door, exclusive for hospital employees, where they had a register clock, where they inserted their employee cards, which would register their in and out time. In his following walk, he had taken along the paper where he had written the notes about the predictions, and when passing again in front of the mentioned marking clock, and *in order not to quit*, he pulled it out of the pocket of his robe, he waited until nobody was at sight, and rapidly inserted the note into the slot and he listened to the characteristic noise of these apparatuses when operating. He pulled out the paper rapidly, hoping that nobody could have observed him. What he had accomplished was not any administrative fault, at all, but he would look ridiculous: a senior citizen playing with such apparatus.

He remained seated in his armchair, in deep concentration, out of his reality, remembering his experience, so to allow the flow of all the details of his past experience, into his memory. When he recovered his consciousness, half an hour had passed over. At that point, he began to think about the consequences of so transcendental proof. Without a doubt, a graphologist (all of them, that were necessary) would be able to confirm and to present his certification, with all certainty, that the age of that paper was, at least, ten years old, and that the data that appear in the paper was written in that same time lapse. And finally that the seal, that covered the text part, indicated, – without doubt –, the veracity of Iturralde's testimony. That earth-shattering paper contained not only one, but two predictions, which meant, the impossibility that both were coincidences. They contained detailed exact data of predictions that came true, according to when they had been stipulated, with ten years of anticipation.

With certainty, he now was sure that other life and ÓMICRON really existed. And that he had gotten in touch with him. He had seen and chatted with his deceased relatives. He had, in like manner shared together with his friendly classmates, Jai Alai players, scientists and musicians. The *giant* characters of all his passions joined together in the same place, and he had gotten in touch with them, also. Verifiable, from the medical point of view, the event did not last for more than two terrestrial minutes. But so many surprising situations happened in that emotive lapse. What experience! Of course, that without the aforementioned aged proofs, but capable of being authenticated, Iturralde would have taken the experience like a fantastic dream, but only that.

I will be the most famous world character, of any epoch! All astronauts that landed on the moon, will be forgotten. In like manner: Edison, Newton, Einstein, etc., they will not be able to compete with my feat. It does not exist anybody that could demonstrate that afterlife exists! Nobody has ever come back, not even the very Houdini, who promised to accomplish it, if it was possible!

Iturralde began to think about all of the advantages that fame could provide; because, no doubt, he will become very famous. He would travel around the world, – first class flights –, and cruisers also in a big way. He would stay at the most luxurious hotels. In relation to his new acquisitions of properties; a big and luxurious house at Chapultepec's Hills, or in some Golf Club, he would learn how to play golf, he always had felt it like playing, – there is where to find contacts to do business –, without forgetting the acquiring, of course, of a house at the West Coast of the United States: San Francisco, Carmel, Monterey? The last few years of his life would be spent at the Mecca of Jazz (what little is still left), that is, close to Los Angeles. He would visit places where live music is played nightly. He would attend all the Jazz festivals; Newport, Monterey and the ones in Europe, Japan and any other place. What a goodbye to life, enjoying, in person, to his *giant* musicians, still alive!

All new furniture, needless to say. It would be necessary to visit these locations, in order to, make an appropriate and calm decision. Referring to automobiles, it would be necessary to stop by at several auto dealers, such as; Porsche, BMW or Mercedes and to drive them, and to feel them. His present-day clothes, will be donated to people in need. He would buy, absolutely everything, first hand, at outstanding expensive stores, not in any commercial malls. He would change his ordinary Citizen watch, for a Rolex. He would buy expensive jewels for his wife. He would be able to buy several stocks in the Stock Market. To his children and grandchildren he will give them, as a present, large sums of money, trips and expensive gifts. He will be able to experience what millionaires feel; without thinking twice, he will take out his credit card and buy all that he can come up with.

And that way he continued thinking, being frank, Iturralde already got sick and tired, of being himself, monetary speaking, somewhat restricted. Always taking care of buying the food that was less expensive, eating previous days' leftovers. Buying food on: *Wednesdays of plaza,* where the supermarket had some merchandise at a better price than normal, thus limiting his purchase to foodstuff that had more accessible prices. Once in a blue moon, he would buy some special item that he does not considers it to be, an excessive expense. Referring to the gas monthly expense, in order to reduce it, he installed thrifty water showers, and also, turning off the gas water heater during the few trips that he experienced. He substituted all the filament light bulbs for the new energy savers, whose proportionate light is insufficient to illuminate well his surroundings, although they save electricity. In order to save more, in the consumption of the computer screen, he saved money by putting it into hibernation state, if in five minutes it is not utilized. He traveled only, by means of the airplane tickets, that come by invitation by his children. Being forced to preserve an automobile, eight years old, which no longer is passing the verification tests, therefore he will not be permitted to use his car one day of the week.

Regarding his wife, practically since he got married, she always has contributed to the family living expenses: preparing my children's classmates for their English exam, selling clothes, silver jewelry, and I no longer remember what else. That´s enough! I am going to thank all her help dearly, providing her with journeys and jewels. The ones that she never thought she could have, the ones that she wants.

That's sufficient! More than enough! Now to live life as a millionaire. The few years that remain of my life. I will appear in the front pages of the principal U.S. and world magazines, as well as in the first pages of important daily newspapers. Probably even in so important magazines such as; *Scientific American* will publish reports about his great feat. I will be requested to be interviewed, and to dictate lectures at universities, radio and television – around the world –. I will be able to collect stratospheric fees. Impossible to predict what the opportunities will be!

Great wealth, rather sooner than later, with plenty of probability (certainty), that I would become avaricious, frivolous, it will change my behavior to the worse, etc. I am only giving consideration to what the riches could bring, and I am already braking the spout out of control. What dreadful power of corruption money has!

Suddenly he stopped that train of thought. Am I, at my age, actively thinking, of committing treason to what I managed to stand for, during the seventy five years of my life, Iturralde reflected?

What I, after that fantastic experience that I was so lucky to experience, did not learn absolutely anything?

Besides, although ÓMICRON had not said that the information provided was personal and confidential, Iturralde felt that to divulge such information with the intention of that it be public in official form, which may be able to cause unsuspected effects, and to have been this the intention of Ómicron, he would have requested so, specifically to Iturralde. Therefore, the correspondent divulgation, without concrete authorization, would be an unethical action. Also he thought from the practical side, I do not desire, in the least, that ÓMICRON may dislike me. He will certainly congratulate me to have done the right thing.

In this way, the only being that has returned from death, and from a mind-bending galactic experience, kept his normal life, without divulging his experience to anybody, knowing almost exactly what is awaiting him when he dies. Iturralde presupposes, than only writing a novel with regard to this marvelous adventure, will not cause, it the least, any separation with ÓMICRON. So, he writes it. This is the novel that you have in your hands.

Printed in the United States
By Bookmasters